Totally Bound Publishing books by Aliyah Burke:

Through the Fire
Seducing Damian

Code of Honour
A Marriage of Convenience
The Lieutenant's Ex-Wife
A Man Like No Other
When Stars Collide

In Aeternum
Casanova in Training
Harbour of Refuge
Protected by Shadows

Interludes
Temporary Home
Alone With You

I0542507

What's Her Secret?

PRECONCEPTION

ALIYAH BURKE

Preconception
ISBN # 978-1-78184-751-0
©Copyright Aliyah Burke 2014
Cover Art by Posh Gosh ©Copyright February 2014
Interior text design by Claire Siemaszkiewicz
Totally Bound Publishing

Published in 2014 by Totally Bound Publishing, Newland House, The Point, Weaver Road, Lincoln, LN6 3QN, United Kingdom.

Totally Bound Publishing is an imprint of Total-E-Ntwined Limited.

PRECONCEPTION

Dedication

Thanks to all my readers who never fail to make me smile with their lovely emails and notes. I wouldn't be where I am today without all y'all. To my husband who is always supportive, no matter where in the world he is. I love you. And as always, my heartfelt thanks to the men and women who selflessly serve their country so that we may be safe. God Bless you and your families!

Chapter One

"I need your help, Carolyn!"

Carolyn Trufant nearly dropped the crystal vase she was filling in the sink. "What's wrong, Jasmine?"

Cars honked. People yelled. The sounds of a busy metropolis's downtown reverberated through the phone line. *Where is she?*

"Help me, please!"

She set the vase down, struggling to hear and decipher the rest of what Jasmine was saying. "I can't hear you."

"…meet me, please."

"Jasmine?" Her voice rose a few notches. "Where do you want me to meet you?"

"Come down to Atlanta, *please*. Meet me where I told you I first visited when I got here. At ten p.m. please, tomorrow. I'm…really scared." The call went dead.

Shit. Carolyn's hands shook like leaves in a stiff breeze. She hung her head and tried to control her racing, out of control emotions.

What could she do? What *should* she do would be a better question.

I have to help her. There's no way I am going to lose her after just finding her.

Caro stroked a finger along the silken petals of the flowers she'd received moments before her sister had called. She loved the variety in the mixture of flowers. *Of course I have to go.*

Allowing herself one more inhalation of the fragrant floral blooms, she swept her gaze around the room, ensuring all items resided in their proper place. Then she went to her office and booked herself a flight to Atlanta.

That evening, once supper had been eaten and cleaned up after, she curled up on one end of her sofa, tucked her feet beneath her and stared through the window of her Madison, Wisconsin, apartment.

She closed her eyes and her thoughts drifted to Jasmine. Her sister. More than that. Her twin. A woman she'd met a month and a half ago. Separated at birth and adopted by other families who didn't know about each other. In fact, even the paperwork stated she had no other known siblings.

To say it had been a shock when Jasmine had first contacted her would be the understatement of the year. Caro had been suspicious, hard not to be when she'd received such a call. She'd asked her parents before about siblings and they'd given her the paperwork, which had denied such things. Still, regardless of her doubts, she'd gone and met her in Saint Louis.

There had been no denying it the moment she'd laid eyes on Jasmine. They'd spent the weekend catching up and learning about one another. Since then they'd exchanged some calls and had discussed having another 'sister' weekend soon. But never a call for help.

She walked to the large window and stared over the twinkling lights of her city. "Never a call with someone sounding so scared either." Caro rested her head against the glass and sighed.

Concerned, she made her way and packed her carry-on. She didn't expect to stay all that long but could take a bit of time off if needed since she had plenty of accumulated days. Lifting the receiver to her landline, she sat on the edge of her bed. She sucked on her lip as she dialed a memorized number. Yes, it was programmed but she did it this way to give herself a bit more time. Not much, true, but anything would be accepted.

"Hello?"

The gentle voice on the other end had her smiling. "Hi, Mama."

"Caro. How are you doing, baby?"

"Fine, Mama. I just wanted to let you and Daddy know I'm taking a short trip." She cleared her throat. "Out of town."

"Hmm. Where to?"

"Down south." She winced, hating the lie she was about to tell. "I have a two week vacation I'm spending in a timeshare."

"Really? You didn't say anything earlier."

Because I didn't know the twin—my twin sister you know nothing about—was going to call me asking for help. "Came up out of the blue. You remember my roommate, Jen? She was going to go but couldn't." She scrunched her eyes and pinched the bridge of her nose. "Just got off the phone with her. I have the time so I figured… Why not?"

More noncommittal noises. "Where down south?"

"Atlanta. I don't have the info yet since she hasn't texted it to me."

"You're leaving when?"

She could see her mother standing there with her head cocked to the side. "Early tomorrow." Late tonight technically but what was one more lie in the grand scheme of things? She was already going to hell.

Her mom, silent for a moment, then made a delicate throat clearing sound. "Have fun and be safe."

"Thanks, Mama." The flush of deceit spread across her neck and face. She despised lying to her parents. "Tell Daddy I say hi. Love to both."

Caro hung up and whimpered.

I feel terrible about this.

Her parents were an amazing couple who'd adopted her and raised her alongside the youngest of their naturally born children. A well-respected couple, they had raised her to understand hard work. When she'd come to Madison for college she hadn't left, and now she worked for the same institution that had supplied her degree. Her boss had been on her case constantly about taking some time off, so she placed a call and left a message on his phone.

Her final call was to her friend who also rented in the same building, Terri Mosse.

"Hello?"

"Hey, Terri. I need a favor."

"Sure thing, babe. What can I do for you?" The blaring music softened. "Everything okay?"

"I'm heading to Atlanta tonight for no more than a couple of weeks."

She whistled low. "Jasmine?"

"Yes." Why did she feel horrible that Terri knew but not her parents?

"You are stressed. What happened?"

"I don't know. She's frightened out of her mind. Asked me to help her." She rubbed the back of her neck. "I can't ignore her. She's my twin."

"I'm not judging, babe. You need to go, go. I will take care of your place. When should I expect you back?"

She pursed her lips. "Not sure. I'm giving myself two weeks if she needs help getting back on her feet. No more than that I wouldn't imagine."

"Your plans change, you let me know."

"I will."

"Caro?"

"Yes, Terri?" She carried her bag to the door.

"Be careful, yeah?"

"I will." They hung up and she pocketed her phone.

She left her apartment, alarm set and door locked, before making her way to the front where she waved for a taxi.

Guilt nagged her as she settled against the leather seat. Her parents—adoptive some may call them, she called them her parents—deserved better than this. They loved her as much as their other children. She'd never felt like she didn't belong in the family. This lying to them was ripping at her gut.

Yes, she could tell them but when she'd asked about what they knew in regards to her birth parents or if she had blood siblings there had been pain in their eyes. She despised hurting them and so when Jasmine had first contacted her, she'd kept it to herself. And the first meeting. Partly to protect them—if she hadn't gotten along with Jasmine, only Caro would have been hurt.

May not have been the smartest thing to leave without telling them exactly where I was going.

She sat up a bit more as the cab drew to a halt before the Dane County Airport below the Delta sign. Passing the driver as she exited, she handed him a bill. "Keep the change."

"Thank you."

She smiled and walked inside to the first kiosk, bag on her shoulder. Before long she had her boarding ticket and was making her way through to security and on to her gate.

Seated in first class, she used the pillow and blanket provided after storing her bag. She closed her eyes and waited for them to take off, alone in her row. She'd raised the rest between the seats.

The flight was uneventful and she woke with the announcement of flight attendants preparing the cabin for landing. She watched the night lights of Atlanta come into view as they approached the airport.

As they taxied to the terminal gate, she withdrew her bag from beneath the seat ahead of her, her nerves suddenly going wonky. She chewed on the side of her lip and wished that she had her papers—she made origami swans when she got stressed or nervous. As a child she'd read *Sadako and the Thousand Paper Cranes* and had created a thousand of her own and hung them up in her room. It was the only shape she could make but she had the ability to create them from any papers.

The seatbelt light blinked off and she gained her feet, swung her bag in front of her and disembarked. Once firmly in the airport, she sidestepped an employee then sent Terri a text before striking out.

She waited for a taxi and gazed around taking it all in. The night was warm, despite it being autumn.

"The Marriott on Peachtree," she informed the driver as he held the door for her.

"Yes, ma'am."

It didn't take long after arriving for her to secure a room and ride the elevator up to it on the thirty-fourth floor. Bag on the bed, she went to the window and stared out. The golden dome of the capital shone brightly against the night skyline.

* * * *

She spent the next day touring the Underground and sampling Coca-Cola in flavors she'd never imagined. Dinner she ate at one of the restaurants in the hotel then at nine she took a taxi to where Jasmine had told her she'd first visited when she'd moved to the capital city.

Caro got out, paid her fare and strolled into the downtown shopping complex. After making her way to the bookstore she grabbed a small table in the café and sipped the coffee she'd ordered.

A few minutes before the allotted meeting time a woman with a large hat and big sunglasses swept into the seat across from her. The items were removed and Caro frowned. Jasmine.

"Jasmine, what is going on? No more of this cryptic talk."

Jasmine held up a finger then went to order a drink and muffin. Caro stared at her twin. They didn't much look alike currently. Sure there were, of course, similarities but Jasmine's hair was pink—bright pink—now and styled, short and spiky. Her clothing... *I wouldn't be caught dead in that.*

Her skintight jeans looked uncomfortable. The stilettos, while extremely nice, were black as was the tight leather jacket she had on, its numerous zippers catching then reflecting the overhead lights.

Jasmine was hiding something. Granted, she didn't know her all that well, but Caro wasn't about to ignore her suspicions. Her sister returned, hips swaying with every step and sat.

There had been no hug or even a half-hearted attempt at one. Caro drummed her fingers along the rim of her plain coffee and watched Jasmine drink the concoction she had. "Well?" Caro prompted.

"I'm in trouble." Her fingers clenched on the cup. "There are some guys after me."

Unease skittered up her spine. "For what? What do they want and who are the 'guys' that are after you?"

Brown eyes met hers. "Really bad guys, Caro. I didn't want to bring you in but"—she glanced around again—"I hoped you wouldn't mind going with me to talk to the cops." A shrug. "Cop. The one who I've been…dealing with. In fact I'd like you to go for me so I can take care of some things I can't do with five-oh around."

Holding up her hand, Caro shook her head. "What did you do? And what makes you think I would go as you."

"I just told what I saw. It was against a crime boss. His men want to kill me so I can't testify against him."

Crime boss? She had a sinking feeling. "You want me to go in your place to meet some cop?" *I need as much information as I can get here.*

"Officer Declan McBride."

She rolled her eyes and Caro got the feeling these two didn't get along all that well.

"And what, he doesn't believe you?"

Her twin shrugged. "We aren't what you could call the best of friends. He doesn't like me and… Let's just say the feeling is mutual." She drank. "The problem also is he has…certain views about how I am and may not be inclined to believe I will be there to testify."

Caro kept her expression composed. She knew Jasmine's adoptive parents had died and she'd been their only child so when they'd gone, she'd had no one. Jasmine's expression was tortured.

Outrage grew inside her, unfolding like angry tendrils. How dare this man treat her sister this way. It had to be horribly frightening to be expected to testify against a crime boss especially feeling so alone.

"Okay, I'll go in your place. I'll help you, whatever you need. He can think what he wants, we're sisters. Twins. It's what we do for one another. I'll go and you get your stuff done." She finished her coffee. "When and where?"

"Thank you!" Jasmine smiled brightly and touched Caro's hand. "We can do lunch after, it shouldn't take too long. Tomorrow morning. I'm going to need you to hang with him for a short time so I can get a few things taken care of. Things I can't do with a cop hanging around me. But I think if everyone is thinking you're me and I'm, meaning you, are with the cops I can get this stuff done. Then I'll come back and we'll trade off again." She wrote an address down on a napkin and slid it over to her. "We should switch bags as well in case he wants your — my — ID."

Caro hesitated. Give up her bag? *Is this legal?* "Is this why you wanted to meet tonight? Like this? You're scared?"

An indescribable emotion filled her features and Caro had that uncertainty again. Jasmine nodded and ate some of her muffin. "I figured they were listening to me and wouldn't know where I was talking about. I wanted to get your help before I went back to the cops." She fidgeted.

Caro waited a while then finally said, "Why don't you leave if you'd prefer not to be out. Do you have a place to go where you feel safe?" She bit her lip and slid her bag to her twin.

"I do. That's part of what I have to resolve on my own. It's a small hostel but I blend in there. I'm safer there than I would be with the cops. This crime boss has a long reach and I would just assume to not be in his way if he tries to reach out and touch me." She stood. "I have to go. See you tomorrow." She donned her hat and glasses before walking off. Halfway to the door, she wheeled back around. "Thanks for coming."

Caro gave a slight nod and waved. *I should be able to just relax if this only takes until tomorrow. She feels safer away from the cops. Perhaps this one is just incompetent in his job. If that's the case we can always ask for another to be assigned. Something has her spooked.* On her feet she grabbed her cup and the items Jasmine hadn't disposed of. Caro grabbed Jasmine's bag and left to hail another cab.

* * * *

This is a shitty day! Declan McBride swore again as he whipped the vehicle around the corner. He slammed his hand on the dash.

"Get out of the way! There's a reason I have this fucking cherry bar on top."

People didn't seem to care and by the time he had made it around the corner he was not any happier. He parked and climbed out, donning his hat. Gazing around, he frowned as he strode toward the store. The message had said she would be waiting for him.

This woman will be the death of me. Because I may very well kill her myself before they get a hold of her.

Jasmine Hoyer. A woman they were supposed to keep safe before the trial. *A pain in the ass is more like it.* She wouldn't do as they advised her, running as often as she could from them and the protection they were there to provide.

When his lieutenant had told him to meet her, he'd refused. "Send someone else," he'd barked. "I'm tired of dealing with her and her spoiled antics. She's made it clear she doesn't want our protection. There are plenty of people in this city who *would* like mine. I'm not wasting my time."

He snorted. Declan nodded with a smile to a little boy who waved at him. His comments hadn't gone over at all. "Which explains why I'm here to meet this obnoxious, spoiled…" He shook his head.

Ten steps from the entrance a scream pierced the air, remarkable considering the level of noise in the area. Immediately, he turned in that direction and started shoving through the crowd.

He reached the woman at the same as another officer. Declan froze. Jasmine. Not the short pink spiked hair, tight clothes wearing Jasmine. But it was her. Which meant she was about to try to slip away, yet again.

"You got this?" he asked the young officer.

"Yes."

"Good." He began across the street holding out his hand to slow cars so that he could progress. "Jasmine!" He made sure his voice carried over the din.

Her head rose as she looked around, finally focusing in his direction. To his left the sun glinted off something and his gut screamed a warning. He ran directly at her, tackling her to the ground as the first shots rang out. Her bag scattered as they hit.

Pandemonium erupted around them. She lay beneath him, eyes wide.

"Damn it, Jasmine!"

He called it in and scanned the area for the shooter. Every fiber in him wanted to chase this person down but his orders were clear. Keep her safe and alive.

She struggled beneath him so he got to his feet then hauled her up as well. *Shit! I have no clue where they went or what they looked like.* He scowled at the woman who continued to tug against him.

"Let go of me!"

"Hold still, Jasmine. I'm in no mood."

She pulled against his hold, but he ignored her, talking to the cops who had arrived.

"I'm not Jasmine. My bag!" She yanked against him trying to get to the spilled items.

"What?" He glared down at her. "What is your problem?"

"I'd just as soon as not lose my things! That's what," she snapped.

"McBride!"

Declan looked up to see his lieutenant pushing through. "LT. What are you doing here?"

The man looked at the woman beside him and back to him. "On my way to a meeting when I heard your call." The man coughed and patted his pockets. "Bring her to my office." LT waved one meaty hand then walked away.

"Let's go," he barked. "You heard LT."

"He's not my lieutenant. What if something stolen from it while you had me pinned on the sidewalk beneath you?" Fury drenched each word that spilled from her mouth.

He crossed his arms and stared down at her before turning his gaze to the surrounding area. "And for your information, you were beneath me because I saved your ungrateful ass from being shot. So... You're welcome."

Her eyes widened. "I'm welcome? I'm welcome?" Her voice eclipsed a pitch he wasn't sure anyone could reach and he winced.

"What's wrong? Did you have a few more drop phones in there to keep us chasing our tails as we try to protect you? If that's what you're worried about being taken I can't say I'm sorry."

Her brow converged but he ignored it. She wasn't about to pull another fast one on him. "I don't care."

"You have this all wrong," she said, tugging against his grip. She gazed behind him, paused, then struggled again.

"Do I?" He faced her fully, getting up in her personal space until the tips of his steel-toed boots rested against the toes of her—interestingly—light blue tennis shoes. "Really? Tell me what I have wrong, Jasmine Hoyer. Do enlighten me. While I see you lost that horrid pink hair and tight clothing, which I am assuming was yet another attempt to sneak away, you're still you."

For a moment, she seemed confused then that damn cool arrogance he was used to and expected from her crossed her features. Declan guided her to his car and held the back seat door open. "I'm tired of running after you. Personally, I don't give a damn if you don't want us around. I don't want to be around you either but orders are orders. I'm tired of it all and tired of the chaos that comes from your selfish actions."

She glared at him, eyes fiery with defiance. Blood resided on her face but if it stung or she was bothered by it, she never let it show. He made a note to get it checked out back at the station.

"This was my fault?" she asked, aghast.

"You're the one with people trying to kill them."

"Sure about that?" she snarked.

He rolled his eyes. "Get in."

"Why? Am I under arrest?"

He ground his teeth and prayed for patience. Yes, he'd love to arrest her. "No, I'm taking you to the station per LT's request. Get. In."

"Would a please kill you?"

"Probably," he grumbled. "Get in...please." It would be hell to unclench his jaw.

"Better be clean back here." Reluctance was stamped all over her body as she slid into the seat and crossed her legs.

Declan slammed the door, a bit harder than necessary, he'd admit that. "This woman..."

"McBride!"

He turned and hid the sneer. *Can my day get fucking worse? I now have to deal with this prick?* Detective Lance Baldwin. Everything about this man just rubbed him wrong. From the way he styled his hair, to the ever-present smirk, which told everyone that Lance believed himself above them, to the custom-made suits he wore. Italian silk. All of it made Declan want to push him into something dirty. Or burn the suit. With the man in it. The detective's smugness smacked him before the man had actually arrived.

"Yeah, Baldwin?" He opened the driver's door and put one foot inside.

"Hear you've been having trouble keeping an eye on your witness."

He eyed him carefully. "Nothing better to do than check up on me? I mean, perhaps you should be out doing some detective work and find the perp who decided to open fire down here."

The man rolled a toothpick he'd put in his mouth. "Heard you were on scene. Couldn't catch him?"

Declan gave a feral grin. "Not a good day to—"

Pop. Pop. Pop. Pop. Pop.

The gunshots spurred them both into action. Baldwin hit the ground while Declan dove into his car, hollering, "Get down!"

Glass shattered around him and he swore as Jasmine screamed bloody murder.

"Go. Go. Go!" Baldwin hollered as he rolled and came up running in the other direction. Toward the shots. The same direction Declan would be going if…

If not for Jasmine.

He readjusted and got them headed away, gunning the engine. "Are you okay?"

Declan repeated his question three times. All of which got zero response from her. He couldn't see her. Whipping into a lot, he then threw the car into park and turned around. She lay slumped in the footwell, blood trickling down the side of her face.

Shit. Shit. Shit!

Calling it in, he raced to the nearest hospital, then screeched to a halt and jumped out. Two nurses waited with a gurney. He yanked open the back door and hauled her out. She lay unresponsive as he placed her on the stretcher.

"You can't park there," one person said.

"I am not leaving her. Move!"

They wheeled her in and he grabbed a security guard as he passed him. "Park my car to the side and bring me the keys."

He stood in the operating room as they worked on her and cursed himself. This was crazy. If he was going to be charged with keeping her alive, which it appeared he was going to be, he had to do it in a place where he could control the surroundings. More so than here anyway.

* * * *

Declan gazed up from where he sat, hand on his pistol—cleared from the holster—when the door to her room swung open. The scowl on LT's face was thunderous. Behind him—his heart sank—came the woman prosecuting the case, a woman in a severe business suit. Jacquelyn Ashcraft. Assistant District Attorney. His ex-wife.

She ran her vibrant green gaze over him and shook her head. "No manners, McBride? You used to stand when a woman walked in the room."

He scratched his stubble and tapped his sidearm against his leg. When the nurse entered he rose and smirked at the frown Jacquelyn shot him.

"She was lucky," he said when just the three of them remained in the room with the still sleeping Jasmine. "They're getting bolder."

"I can't win with a dead witness," Jacquelyn snapped.

He clenched his jaw to keep his comment inside.

"I'm sure death would be an inconvenience to Ms Hoyer as well," LT said with an eye roll. LT, it appeared, had no problem voicing his opinion.

"Whatever," she replied. She glared at both of them. "Keep her alive or it's your asses." She departed the room with the same cold precise steps with which she'd entered.

Damn woman gave him frostbite. Declan readjusted in his chair.

LT ran a hand over his hair. "Suggestions?"

"Let me put her somewhere."

"Like?"

"Nope. Somewhere only I know. I'll leave you a number to call when she's needed in court. Just give us forty-eight hours' notice.

LT watched him with dark brown eyes. "You can't stand her."

He shrugged. "There are a lot of people I'm not a fan of. Doesn't mean I won't protect them with any less passion."

"You're a damn good cop, Declan. I'm not implying otherwise. How many times have I encouraged you to take the detective's exam?"

"Many. And my answer will be the same. I like being on the streets. Walking a beat. I don't want to be a detective."

LT harrumphed. "Discussion for another time." His lieutenant held his gaze. "You sure you want to do this?"

"Nope, but it's the smartest thing. I can't imagine it will be fun being in close quarters with her."

LT smirked. "You never know."

He snorted. "Not likely." And yet, he couldn't deny his body responded to her feistiness with a fervor he wasn't pleased with. More so just since today. He hadn't felt it before, but from his first touch on her in the street earlier, his cock had jumped in with his own opinion. There was something different. It didn't matter—he was in control of his body, not the other way around.

"Give me the number."

Reaching into the front pocket of his uniform shirt, he withdrew his little notepad. After a few strokes of his pen he ripped the sheet free and handed it over.

"No name?"

"Nope. Just tell whoever answers she's needed and I'll be there within forty-eight with her in tow."

"This is a DC number."

Declan shrugged and stared at the woman in the bed. Right now she looked lost and small. *All of which changes when she's awake.*

"We'll leave when she wakes."

LT put a smoke in and sighed. "Be careful." The man played with his lighter but never once lit the cig dangling from his lower lip.

"Always am."

Moments later, he and Jasmine had the room to themselves. He settled back and waited. Declan needed to use this time to try to figure out a way to stay ahead of her. They'd butted heads many of times. This was different, though.

The Kazakova crime family was nothing to scoff at. They did what they did and not a single one of the witnesses against the family tended to make it to court, so they were continually freed. Jasmine and one other were their last chance.

Chapter Two

Caro hurt. Flashes bombarded her and she jerked up at the memory of being shot. Pain smacked her and she cried out.

"Want me to call the doc?" The voice—deep and, dare she think it despite the pain, arousing—had her looking to see who'd spoken.

Him? He's still here with me? Her cop. Declan McBride.

He sat there, long legs stretched out before him, wearing the hell out of his uniform. Cops didn't normally do anything for her but this one... Something different entirely.

"What are you doing here?"

He quirked an eyebrow. "Protecting you."

"Isn't that how I got shot?" Okay, so perhaps that was a low blow but she wasn't about to roll over for him. *Then again, that could prove to be fun.*

Her mind had figured it out. Jasmine had wanted this cop to latch onto her more than originally stated. She gazed at the table and saw Jasmine's ID. *She had no intention of swinging back by soon and us doing lunch. I'm a fool. I let her dupe me.*

Guilt nagged her, though. Jasmine had been alone for so long. She had to help her. Jasmine had said she had a place to hide. *This may be stupid of me to continue but I promised I would help her and that's exactly what I'm going to do.*

"You want the doc?" His tone was angry.

"No."

"Great. Let's go."

Her eyebrows shot up. "Go?" She looked down at her body. "Where am I going in a hospital gown?"

"Doc said you could leave when you woke. You're awake. We can go."

Not one for bedside manner, I see. She gazed beyond the window. Night had fallen. "Again. Go where?" She turned her attention to him as she waited for his answer.

"Somewhere you'll be safe."

Safe. A word she liked. She'd never been shot before and it wasn't an experience she cared to repeat.

"I don't have a choice, do I?"

Anger darkened his blue-green eyes. "I would have no problem walking out that door and never laying eyes on you again. I have my orders."

He and Jasmine must hate one another. She left the bed and stomped over to him. He stared up at her from where he sat, his expression daring her. To do what, she wasn't sure but she read the challenge in his gaze.

"Then do it." She dared him.

Declan unfurled from the seat to stand over her. *Lord, he's big.* Before, she'd been a bit too freaked to truly admire the man before her. Now, she took it all in. Took all of *him* in. Six-five, broad shoulders, narrow waist. Powerful. Short black hair highlighted the chiseled, nearly harsh features. His nose had a bump indicating a previous break. Firm lips, which she — for a second only — wondered what they would be like upon hers.

"I have my orders." He raked his gaze over her. "It's just going to be you and me. No more games. No more stealing cars, no more lies. And that includes this, 'I'm not Jasmine' thing you spouted."

Stolen cars? What the hell kind of person was her twin?

"I need to make a call."

"To who? Your dealer?" Derision drenched his questions.

She just reacted, her hand rushed toward his face. Declan snagged her wrist and jerked her close to him. Heat swirled in his eyes and she lost herself momentarily in their depths.

"I do *not* do drugs." Fury rocked through her.

A scoff. "You won't be where we're going, that's for sure. Put some clothes on or did you want to go that way?"

She couldn't believe how little he thought of her — *Jasmine. Me for now.* Part of her thought it would be wise to tell him exactly who she was. At least try to get him to understand. The recollection of Jasmine's face had her swallowing it. She could do this.

Caro backed away and found a bag holding her clothing. She ducked in the bathroom and put her attire on. Staring at her reflection, she chewed on her lip. *Think like Jasmine.*

Not an easy feat. Especially given what he — Declan 'hottie' McBride — kept informing her when he lashed accusations at her — Jasmine's character.

"I can do this. It shouldn't take long."

Hopefully it wouldn't be longer than her two weeks. She needed to call and cancel her cards. "Damn it. What am I doing?"

She splashed water on her face then dabbed it dry with a towel.

Bam. Bam. Bam. His heavy pounding startled her. "Hurry up."

Feeling brave behind the door, she stuck her tongue out at him. "I'm coming," she cried back. *All I have to do is channel the twin I really don't know to fool a cop who's hot as fuck and apparently has a hard-on for me — Jasmine — and not in a good way. Also he seems to be a damn good cop so I'll have to really sell this switch.* She tried for a smile only to grimace. *Should be a piece of cake.*

One last fortifying breath and she opened the door, stepping out to face her fate.

"What's your rush?" she snapped.

"You need to pack a bag."

Panic flared. She had no idea where Jasmine — she — lived. "So take me there." She left the room ahead of him. "Excuse me," she said when someone bumped her.

They kept going without a word. She glanced back to see Declan watching her, a furrow in his brow.

"What?" Christ, had she fucked up already?

"When did you get manners?"

Jesus, Jasmine. What kind of person are you? "Blame the drugs," she said continuing on and entering the elevator.

He trailed her in, and the space shrank with his presence. She wasn't sure what was wrong with her. All she could envision was her and Declan lying in a bed — or anywhere — naked, limbs entwined.

Gulping, she put her hands in her pockets and discovered a folded sheet of paper. *The person who bumped into me.*

He checked her out and led the way into Atlanta's night. A black Crown Vic sat there off to the side and a portly man climbed out. Declan and the other man talked with bent heads. She faced away from them and withdrew the note.

I'm safe. There are some things I have to attend that couldn't be done if I was in police custody, like I mentioned before. Please trust me on this, I know you don't have a reason to, but I'm begging you to just trust me. So sorry you were shot at, I had no idea that would happen and glad you are okay. He'll keep you safe so long as you stay with him. Whatever you do, stay with him, Carolyn. C U at court, I promise I'll be there. Thanks, sis.

Caro shoved it back in her pocket and mulled over telling him once more.

"Come on!" he barked behind her.

Flaring her nose as she turned, she then walked over and got in the back of the car. Declan followed her in. Being with him in the elevator had been bad enough, but in the back seat of a car... Oh the drugs... It *had* to be the drugs.

Caro sat pressed against the door and gasped in outrage when he snapped a handcuff on one wrist. She jerked only to see the other end attached to him.

"Are you serious?" She jangled her arm and his subsequently.

He put her wrist down. "Until I get you to where we're going, consider us inseparable."

She clamped her lips on the words she longed to spew at him. Caro stared through the window and stewed in silence. They parked before a run-down apartment complex.

"Let's go."

Let's go. Come on. Can you say anything else? She trailed him out, careful not to touch him more than absolutely necessary.

He stared at her and she just lifted her chin. She had no idea where to go so she had to appear uncooperative. Not a stretch to be sure. He scoffed and led the way to the third floor. When they paused before a door he stared at her. "Well?" he asked.

"Well what?" she sassed.

"Open the door."

"I don't seem to have my keys. Maybe I could pick it with my pinky nail."

They glared at one another for a bit. "Where's your super live?"

She studied her nails, keeping mum. He glared then withdrew his phone. She ignored the lingering pain in her head and appeared as bored as she could make herself.

"It's McBride. Call Hoyer's super and have him come open the door. She doesn't have any key on her. We're there now." He shoved his phone back in his pocket.

Caro hesitantly leaned against the wall. A tall, reed thin Middle Eastern man strode up a short time later, glaring at her the entire walk, then unlocked the door.

"She being arrested again?" the man asked, disapproval stamped all over his tone.

"Nope," Declan said. "She was shot today."

The super's snort told her it wasn't a surprise to him, and Caro realized Jasmine wasn't well liked here either. They entered, Declan first, keeping her behind him, his weapon drawn, but all she focused on was how nice he smelled. Dark. Woodsy. Masculine. *Yummy.*

He stopped so abruptly she ran into his back. *Yes, yummy and hard.* The man had no give on him at all. They'd checked the entire place. He faced her. After digging in his pocket, he lifted their joined wrists and unlocked his end of the cuff, but didn't release it.

"Look at me."

She did. Her heart pounded harder as his blue-green eyes focused on her. It would be so easy to rise up on her tiptoes and press their lips together.

So must be the meds. "What?" *Wait, is that my voice all thready and breathy?*

His gaze briefly dropped to her mouth. "Pack a bag. Be quick about it and do *not* try to escape."

Whatever moment she'd imagined in her mind vanished with his words and tone. She stepped away only to pause and flick her look from the cuff on her wrist to his hand on the other end. Eventually he let go.

She went to the bedroom, doing her best not to think what it would be like—and how easily she would agree—if he used those cuffs on her to keep her in bed. *Guess I should have had sex before I came down here.* She gazed around her and didn't bother stopping the need to curl her lip at the décor. Gaudy. Opposite of how her place was. She located a bag and scowled at the options in the closet. She eyed the dresser and shook her head.

No way in hell I'm wearing her underwear and bras.

"What's the hold-up?"

She glanced at the silver dangling from her limb and faced him. "Where are you taking me?"

"Somewhere safe."

"So buy me some clothes there."

"Buy you some?" He sounded incredulous.

"Yes." She lifted her chin. "You refuse to tell me where we're going, well fine. You can buy me stuff there."

She went to the bathroom and suppressed a shudder. No way could she live like this. Cleaning was necessary. She dropped the note in the full trash can, took a few breaths—not too deep because of the smell—then walked out to stand before him.

Declan hooked her to him and led her out to where he then directed the super to lock it up. That Crown Vic waited and he gestured for her to enter first. This ride was silent as well, and when they stopped to get out it was at a parking garage. Her belly clenched with uncertainty when the car drove off, leaving the two of them alone.

"What now?" she asked, proud her voice didn't shake.

"We wait."

She wanted to lie down, her day had been trying. As much as she attempted, she couldn't stop the yawn. He slanted his gaze to watch her but she pretended she didn't see him.

Shortly, a white car with tinted windows pulled up. This time, Declan got in first and she followed him. Another yawn and that was all she knew.

* * * *

Declan looked at the woman who continued to slumber beside him in the airline seat. She'd barely woken to make it through the security checkpoint before she was sleeping again. He understood it, she was exhausted.

There was something about her. Something different from before—he just couldn't quite put his finger on it. Instead of him wanting to get far away from her, she stirred something in him, something fiercely protective, and it made him scowl. He and this woman didn't get along. Case and point. It just wasn't happening.

So, genius, why are you staring at her and contemplating drawing her in closer to you? Declan shook his head at his brain's commentary and tucked the blanket up a bit more.

Maybe it was all their run-ins during this case that had finally got her under his skin in a different way from annoyance. No, that wasn't it. There was attraction there now and she seemed more lost than usual.

As the plane continued on toward their destination, he ran over her file in his head. Parents, deceased. No family. By all accounts she was alone. Yes, she was trouble, he could attest personally to that but maybe, just maybe, now she'd realized how much danger she was truly in.

She stirred and flexed her fingers. The tips brushed against his hand and without much thought he opened his hand and held hers. Her murmur was soft but she settled. Their fingers laced together, Declan made sure their hands were covered by a blanket then he stared up and tried to figure out why he'd decided to do what he was doing.

Once they'd landed and disembarked he led her out into the night, noting her shiver, and bit back his response of how if she'd packed something she could be warmer. They stopped by a Jeep and he unhooked her from the cuff. She looked everywhere but at him.

"This is the safest place for you right now. When the store opens up I'll take you in for some clothing. No more cuffs for if you jump out of the vehicle, that's on you. Got it?"

Her nod was barely there. He strode around and picked the key up from above the front wheel well then slipped behind the wheel. Starting the engine, he smiled as the jacked-up vehicle rumbled to life. Even being back here at this time of the night brought a smile to his face. This was his home and he'd been away far too long.

He drove them through the mountains it was too dark to see, and to his cabin, which sat way back from anything. Jasmine didn't talk and he occasionally checked on her. She sat ramrod straight in her seat — he figured she didn't want to fall. The air bordered on cold but he loved it. After a hot and sweltering summer in Atlanta, this felt amazing.

Turning off on his road, he slowed as they approached his cabin. He parked the Jeep and shut off the engine. A noise caught his attention and he looked to his right, realizing it was coming from Jasmine. Jumping out, he dashed around the Jeep to her side. Her skin was like ice.

Damn it!

He lifted her in his arms and walked into the cabin. A lone light was on and a fire burned in the hearth, offering up warmth to the space. Declan set her on her feet and encouraged her to put her hands near the flames.

"You'll warm up shortly." He kept his words gruff even though he wanted to gather her close and share his heat with her. What had he been thinking? She'd just been shot and he had put her in an open Jeep to go through the Sierra Nevadas at night. *Some cop I am.*

He draped a quilt around her as well then walked away to check out his cabin. All his requests had been met and he was grateful for that. He took the keys along with his bag from the Jeep then made his way back in. Jasmine was sleeping on the floor, the quilt firmly wrapped around her.

Leaving her there for a moment, he put his bag in his room then went to the guest room where he drew back the covers on the bed. Once that was finished, he returned to get her. He crouched down, slid his arms beneath her and lifted. She stirred before she gave a little moan that was like she'd reached out and stroked his cock.

It took him very little time to put her in the bed before covering her up with even more blankets. *Like that's going to stop my imagination.* Declan left the room with very deliberate steps.

* * * *

His night had been rough but he was up again by the time the sky started to lighten. A mug of coffee in his hand, he stood out on his porch, leaning against one of the rails. He didn't hear her, more felt her. One minute nothing, the next she was there.

Declan glanced askew at her as she stood beside him. He swore there was a ghost of a smile on her lips as she gazed about her.

"Where are we?"

Her voice, deep and husky with sleep, shot lead through his cock and he cleared his throat before answering. "Sierra Nevadas. You'll never find your way out so don't even try."

"Right. Am I allowed some coffee or do I need to get down on my knees and beg for it?"

Images of just that flashed through his mind and his dick pressed harder against his jeans. "Help yourself."

She vanished, all the while muttering beneath her breath. He finished his drink and walked inside only to pause. Jasmine wasn't in the kitchen. His place wasn't all that big so he could see most of the living room and from what he could see there, she wasn't in there either.

But when he walked in he saw her, curled up by a window, quilt covering her legs and mug in hand, gaze fixated out on the mountains that surrounded them.

"When you finish," he said, "we'll go to the store. I need staples."

"I'm done." She unfolded herself from the chair and moved in his direction only to bypass him with a wide berth, as if she couldn't stand being in close proximity.

He stood there and listened to her rinse out the mug. Another mystery given the state of her apartment. Jasmine waited for him by the door and it didn't take long for them to be in the Jeep. He handed her one of his old jackets.

She took it without a word and slipped it on. He swore she sniffed it but chalked it up to another delusion. "How's your head feeling?"

"Slight throb. It's fine." She burrowed deeper into his jacket as he drove and the wind poured over them.

He needed to get his truck or put the doors on this one. *Why do I care? If I keep the Jeep maybe she won't try to leave the first chance she gets.*

She didn't speak the entire way to the small town. He parked in front of the store and hopped out. Jasmine followed a bit slower, keeping the jacket tight around her. Heat hit them as they stepped inside and he smiled over the familiar sights and sounds.

"Declan? Declan, is that you?"

"Hey, Martin."

A big man, Martin Slater, strode into view, a smile on his face. They hugged and when they separated, Martin glanced at the woman beside him, a puzzled look taking over his features. "And you are?" he asked.

Jasmine reached out her hand and said, "Caro."

Martin shook it. "Fiancée?"

"Oh God no. We barely get along. He just brought me here for a short visit."

"Martin, will you excuse us for a second?"

"Sure thing." The man had a knowing smile on his face as he walked away. "Come in the back when you're done. I've got some coffee for you."

Alone, he whirled on her. "Caro? What is that about?"

"I'm Caro." She shrugged her shoulders in his large jacket. "Short for Carolyn in case you were wondering. Now" — she turned around, finger pointing out — "where do I shop for clothing?"

After she walked off, he went to find Martin who was leaning against the counter in the back, arms crossed and watching Jasmine, now Caro, shop.

"Thought you said she was Jasmine."

"She's a pain in my ass is what she is."

"I don't know, Caro fits her. She's not like what you said."

"Don't be too sure about that, she's a master at manipulation."

Martin raised a white eyebrow. "Really? That little thing? Your jacket pretty much swallows her up."

"Yes, that little thing." He sat on the counter. "Thanks for setting up my place and having a fire in it."

"No problem. I was glad to hear you were coming back. You've been away for so long."

Declan nodded. The man spoke the truth.

"You two better get your story straight. You know she's bound to run into a few others sooner or later."

Declan knew that. "Yes, I know."

"Why is she shopping? Didn't she bring her own clothing?"

"Nope. Refused to pack a bag."

Martin coughed and turned his head. Declan knew the man was laughing.

"She seems pretty at home in the section she's in."

Declan poured himself another cup of coffee and stirred in a bunch of sugar as he watched her look at jeans. Martin was right, she did appear comfortable there.

"You know, I know that look you're trying to hide, right, son?"

He smoothed out his expression and met Martin's gaze with a raised eyebrow. "Don't go there. This is about protection and nothing else."

"Right, you keep telling yourself that. All those nights, especially once this snow arrives."

Making love to her as the snow fell around them. He shifted on the counter and Martin laughed.

"Stuff it, old man," he snipped, half-heartedly.

"Sure, son, sure. You know you may want to mark your calendar for nine months after this 'visit' out here."

"I am not—" He snapped his mouth shut when she approached.

"How long are you—we staying?"

He admired her catch. "Not sure yet. If you need more we can always come get more."

"Good. I'm ready."

Martin reached out and took the massive pile from her. "Let me help you with that, hon."

"Thank you," she said in a gentle tone.

Declan rolled his eyes and slid off the counter. He noticed there were bras and underwear in her pile as well. Odd she hadn't wanted to bring anything of her own with her. As Martin bagged it, Declan stared at the woman Martin spoke to. Even her voice was a bit different. Why hadn't he noticed that before?

Four bags of clothing plus boots and shoes. Not the kind he would have assumed she would get—instead she'd picked hiking boots and tennis shoes. He hefted three of the bags and left one for her. She smiled at Martin and lifted the final bag before trailing behind him from the store. They went back inside for the needed groceries as well. She threw in a toothbrush, floss and toothpaste along with some other personal items.

"He won't help you," Declan said as he put the items in the back of the Jeep.

"Oh my God, let it go already," she said throwing her hands up in frustration. "I get it. I'm stuck here with you. No one around would dare go against the great Declan McBride. Especially to help someone like me. Let it go. I get it. I'm a pain in your ass and you don't want me around. Like I want to be around you. I'm here, I'll do this and then when we get back to Atlanta, I hope to God I never have to lay eyes on you again. There's no need to constantly remind me how utterly alone and isolated you've made me."

She stomped to the front and climbed in. Declan looked up and saw Martin there with a frown on his face. The old man, one he looked on as a father figure, was disappointed in him. Declan couldn't explain it, it was her—Jasmine, or Caro, however she wanted to call herself—she brought the worst out in him. He waved to Martin and got behind the wheel.

They exchanged no words on the ride back to his cabin. She did help him carry everything in although she left him to put away the groceries as she went to her room with the clothing. He didn't see her until he went to look for her at lunchtime.

"Jasmine."

She didn't even look up. He tried her name two more times with the same result. *Okay, I'll bite and give it a shot.* "Caro," he called.

She looked up instantly. "Yes?"

"Lunch."

She put down the puzzle book she was working on and rose from the chair she'd been in by the window. She had thick socks on her feet and wore jeans and a sweatshirt.

"Do you think you could help me put the top on my Jeep this afternoon? And the doors?"

"Sure." She didn't slow nor did she look back at him.

He walked behind her to the kitchen, where there was soup and sandwiches waiting for them. Declan dished up the soup and watched her sit at the table. He felt bad—he knew he'd hurt her with his earlier comments but damn it, she should have expected it. It wasn't as if she had made any of this easy to begin with.

After they ate, she cleaned up then looked at him. "I'm going to take a shower."

Caro walked into the small bathroom. She just needed a hot shower to warm her up a bit before she went out into the cold. Maybe it would assist her head in feeling less like there was a troop running in formation up there. She turned on the water and stripped off her clothes before stepping into the tub.

The hot water cascaded around her and she groaned in pleasure. Closing her eyes, she let the streams work on the tense aches in her body. She could use a good masseuse but this would work in a pinch.

With a contented sigh, she rubbed the back of her neck and opened her eyes. "Ahhhh!" The scream ripped up from her throat and filled the air.

A large spider sat along the wall. The door burst open as Declan shot through.

"What's wrong?" he demanded.

She met his gaze and damned if the man didn't pause for a moment to run his stare over her naked body. It had to be her imagination that there was a gleam of appreciation in his eyes. The eight-legged creature on the wall moved and she screamed again as she jumped into Declan's arms. He caught her with ease and she had to remind herself to get out of his embrace as well before she... Those feelings weren't anything she needed to think about right now.

"I'll take care of it," he said.

She grabbed a towel, wrapped it around her body and bolted.

Caro sat there, shivering, wrapped by the quilt on the bed when he stepped into the room.

"You can finish your shower."

She lifted her gaze to find him watching her face. "Are there more of them?"

"Not a fan I take it?"

She didn't deign him an answer. He may find this amusing but her heart was pounding so hard she wondered if it wouldn't just burst free from behind her ribs onto the floor.

"It wasn't poisonous."

"Is that supposed to make me feel better?"

"Couldn't hurt."

She scrubbed her hand over her face. Her body wouldn't quit shaking. He beckoned a hand out to her.

"What?"

"Just thought you'd want to finish your shower."

Caro stood and again there went a flare of desire in his gaze. She scrunched her fingers on the towel by her breasts, and made her way behind him to the bathroom. He moved the curtain and she stared at the walls. Clear. She remained immobile while he turned the water back on.

"There you go."

She didn't move until he went by her and closed the door behind him. Then she dropped the towel and hurried back into the water. This time there was no lingering. She washed quick, body tense as could be, and got out just as swiftly. It took her less time to dry off and shove herself back into her attire. With a shudder, she unpinned her hair and allowed it to fall. Only the ends were damp and she didn't much care about that.

Declan watched her from the living room when she stepped from the bathroom. Christ, she was still shaking. Clearing her throat, she made her way in his direction. He arched an eyebrow and held her gaze.

"Thank you."

His eyes moved up and down over her clothed body. "My pleasure."

"Are those things common?"

"My guess is it was trying to get out of the cold. No, that's not to say you need to expect them in your bed at night. I don't think you'll see any more."

Bed. Now she had to worry about them in her bed? Oh, Lordy, she was going to hyperventilate. *This sucks. It's not like it's going to get any warmer outside. It's just about to snow for crying out loud.*

"Great." She walked to the bedroom and picked up her shoes, shook them out and put them on her feet. "I'll never sleep. Not with those big nasty things around."

In the back of her mind, she wanted to focus on why he had looked at her as he had. *Don't need to be thinking on that either. He's a man, a naked woman jumped into his arms. I'm sure it was purely reflex for him to look that way.*

Didn't explain the look in the living room but she had enough on her plate without worrying that there may be something more than animosity between her and Declan McBride. At least he came running when she screamed.

Right, because you're no good to him dead. She snorted and left the bedroom. *I'm no good to him at all. I'm not even Jasmine.*

Chapter Three

The wind whipped around Caro with a biting force she usually experienced during winter in Madison when that blistering cold air came off the lakes. She squinted against it and struggled to snap the final one to secure the top on his Jeep. *At least he knows to put this on and the doors. Not that I see myself going many places but it would have been cold as fuck.* Snow was coming, she could smell it in the air.

His place astounded her. Her kind of living conditions. A cabin, secluded away from everything else around it. Mountains as far as she could see. What had taken him to Atlanta she didn't know but were she him, she would still be living here. Except for the spiders. They didn't need to be anywhere near her.

Finally! The last snap secured, she stepped back and winced as a lance of pain pierced her skull. *This ain't good.* She reached out to stabilize herself against the Jeep but her fingers encountered one hard-bodied man named Declan McBride.

"Shit," she muttered as the ground rushed up to meet her.

She opened her eyes and discovered Declan held her as his long strides ate up the ground. Pushing against his chest, she cleared her throat. "What happened?"

"You passed out." His words were gruff.

"I'm awake now. Want to put me down?"

She couldn't explain her emotional turmoil at being held by this man. He exuded warmth and safety. It confused her. Every single thing about him confused her.

Declan scowled. *He does that a lot.* Still, despite the frown and the attitude of his that screamed 'keep your distance' he carried her in his arms with a gentleness she'd not expect on face value—it belied what he showed the world of his personality. He opened the door and she sighed at the extra warmth that hit her.

He continued to hold her in his arms until he reached the sofa and set her upon the cushions.

"What happened?"

He shrugged out of his leather jacket and tossed it onto a chair, then crouched before her. She focused on his thighs beneath the tight drawn jeans.

He lifted her chin—callused fingers doing unmentionable things to her insides—and held her gaze.

"What happened?"

"I felt dizzy. I'm fine now. We can go put on the doors." She had to get some distance before she did something foolish like kiss the man.

"No."

Damn him. Why was he pretending to be concerned now? Why wouldn't he release her and why the hell was she picturing them having sex beneath this majestic backdrop of the mountains?

"I'm fine."

She tried to move her head away from his touch but he tightened his grip. "Don't worry," she snapped, adding in some bite. "I won't die yet. I know how you need to bring me back alive and your job won't be happy if I kick the bucket."

That did it. He pushed up with a fluid move. "Let's go then."

He walked away and she ignored her internal chastising for being such a bitch to him. All he'd done was show some concern for her. *Damn you, Jasmine, for putting me in this situation.*

Even so, as she returned to the outdoors, she realized she couldn't put the blame on her twin. She was the one who'd agreed to go along with the ruse. No one had forced her to. True, determination to protect her sister and some guilt may have played a part but ultimately, the decision had been hers to make. It wasn't her fault that she had been brought up in a loving home surrounded by supportive family and Jasmine hadn't. Didn't matter, their circumstances easily could have been altered. Caro knew she could have been the baby to go where Jasmine had gone.

She thought more about the note and wondered what Jasmine could be doing. Was she safe? Truly?

A few fat flakes drifted down from the sky when she stepped off the small porch. Without a word she went to Declan's side and waited for him to tell her what to do. It didn't take them long to do it and he directed her with a minimum of words. In fact, it was more that he spoke on installing the first door and she just mimicked her action on the other side. He didn't say anything at all for the second installation.

By the time they had finished, the few flakes had changed to a steady falling. She tipped her head back and allowed the cold to bite into her skin. It revitalized her. She'd always been a fan of winter.

"You should go inside," he said.

She avoided looking at him, just did as he'd said. Once she'd shrugged out of her jacket and hung it on the wooden pegs by the entrance, she saw him through the window as he parked the Jeep in a nearby shed. On his way back to the house, he gathered some more wood.

Determined not to be found staring after him like a lovesick child, she opened the cupboards and tried to find something to make for their evening meal. Even so, she was hard pressed not to ogle the man as he made numerous trips from the woodshed to the cabin's porch.

He was in his element here, she could see that. Although he no longer donned the uniform—which was hot as sin on him—the jeans and flannel fitted him even better. He was a rugged man, no way to hide that aspect. The snow stuck in his short hair and she clenched her hand as the urge to go out there and wipe it away hit her.

"What the hell is going on with me? Why does my body pick now to behave like a horny bunny rabbit? I can't be thinking like this or I'll be humping his leg before nightfall."

She decided to make some biscuits, for they went with everything in her opinion, and took her frustration out on them, working the dough with fierce concentration until she rolled it out and used a glass from the cupboard to cut them before placing them on the cookie sheet. Once twelve sat on the sheet, she slid it in the oven, and checked the time on the wall clock.

They would be done on time with the rest of the meal. Pork chops and macaroni and cheese. She'd found some green beans to add to their supper as well and as she checked them, she lowered the heat slightly on them.

Why isn't he coming inside? Is something wrong?

She set the table and removed items from the oven when he walked in the front. After the door had closed, she stared at him while placing the sheet of biscuits on the hot pad. Then she turned back and withdrew the bubbling macaroni. He no longer stood there when she faced that direction again.

Probably doesn't even want to eat with me. It stung, she wouldn't lie about that, but she was used to eating alone so in the grand scheme of things it wasn't all that big of a deal.

The man she thought about appeared in the kitchen, silent as a wraith. She made one last check of the pork chops before she carried the pan to the table. Declan appeared across from her with the pasta. She went back to the biscuits and placed them in the towel-lined bowl prior to bringing it to the table as well.

When he held a chair she furrowed her brow. He lifted an eyebrow in return and she acquiesced to allow him to seat her, his woodsy masculine scent filling her nose as he moved her closer to the table. Declan sat across from her.

"Thank you."

His rasp skated along her skin. She couldn't believe how much two simple words from him could make her so giddy. *I have got to grow up here—this is like I'm infatuated with him for no particular reason.*

"Sure."

They didn't talk during the meal and that suited her fine. She needed to figure out how to maintain the callous attitude. Her problem—one of them—was that she admired him. He'd put up with what appeared to be hell, her twin. Despite *all* that, he'd ignored his own personal feelings and done what had needed to be done in order to keep her safe. How could she *not* respect that in this man?

He offered to clean up and she retreated to her temporary room. Seated on the bed, awash in the soft light from the lamp, she folded paper and enjoyed the silence as outside the snow fell in thick, heavy flakes, the accumulation beginning to line her windowsill.

No way Jasmine would have handled this. Everything about her is chaotic from her clothing to her apartment. However, for Caro personally, this was heaven—pure and simple.

Before she crawled beneath the heavy quilt to sleep, she left the room to brush her teeth. Declan stepped from the bathroom, clad only in a pair of low riding sweats.

Moisture flooded her pussy as she stared at him. *Oh my God!* He was a freaking work of art. Ridges and planes. Her entire body swayed toward him, responding to his masculinity on a molecular level. Visceral yearning gnawed at her, burned her fingertips, and created an ache deep within her gut.

Hard. Muscled. Tanned. A man unlike any she'd seen before and one who affected her on so many levels. It wasn't sensible, her attraction to him—but it was what it was.

His gaze burned into her and she fought not to squirm beneath it. He stepped to the side and she slid past him, their bodies nearly touching yet not. She inhaled deeply allowing his fragrance—clean and…all about Declan—to flow over her, tantalizing her further.

Once the door had shut behind her she released her shaky breath. She rested against the wood and tried to steady her nerves. It took a bit. *This isn't good. Had I known this was going to be my situation, I would have brought a vibrator to take the edge off while here.*

Who wanted to use plastic when there was a man one door away from her who did this to her? Maybe if she walked into his room and stripped naked he'd do something about this unbelievable amount of arousal he'd created inside her. She snorted lightly and shook her head. *Sure thing, Caro. Bet that would go over real well.*

She took care of her teeth, washed her face, and made her way back to her room. The house was warm and dark, yet she had no problem making it safely. She crawled beneath the bedding before reaching out to click off the light. Madison wasn't loud but this was silence on an eerie scale, almost. She enjoyed it but it wasn't what she was used to.

* * * *

The sound of children woke her. She sat in a rush and winced over another slight pain in her head. Kids? Why was she hearing kids? The curtains in her room had been drawn. She made her way to the window and peered out.

Five kids ran around out there, playing in the snow that had accumulated overnight and continued to fall. Caro looked at the clock and saw it was after noon. *How the hell did I sleep so long?*

She dressed quickly and drew her hair back into a simple ponytail. Tugging up one sock, she opened the bedroom door and stepped out into the hall. With a deep breath, she headed up the hall to see what was going on.

A couple sat in the living room with Declan. All three glanced at her as she entered and she pulled up. The look Declan gave her made her want to pivot around and run all out back to the bedroom. He didn't seem pleased at all. The woman stared at her, mouth in a small 'o' and eyebrows raised, while the man gave her a lewd look.

"Oh, hello," the woman said. "When Martin said you had company I didn't know... Umm... I didn't expect..." she trailed off, her face burning bright red. "I'm sorry, I'm Tasha Harstone."

"Caro." She didn't move any closer. "Sorry to interrupt."

Declan set down his mug and rose. "It's fine. Tasha, Jimmy, this is Caro. They live in town and came out for a visit."

Caro gave a weak smile. "Nice to meet you both."

Jimmy pointed at his head. "What happened to you?"

Shit! The injury was obvious because she had pulled her hair back. She glanced at Declan wanting to follow his lead on this. He gave her a small nod.

"I was shot."

"Oh my God!" Tasha said, covering her mouth. "Around here?"

"Nope," Declan interjected. "I brought her here to recover. That's why you didn't meet her earlier. She's been sleeping it off."

Sleeping it off, like she was an alcoholic or something. Caro bit back her grumble of discontent and let it go. She wanted something to eat but she didn't like how under observation they had her.

"I think I'll go lie back down," she said.

"Have you eaten?" Tasha asked, getting to her feet. "We brought Declan some food and I don't mind making you a plate. We could get to know one another more. It would be nice to have another woman around to talk to."

Caro stepped forward. "That would be nice. He's not much of a conversationalist."

Together they went to the kitchen, Caro ignoring the warning glare from Declan.

Declan had stared at Caro as she'd walked by him with Tasha. Both women were of average height, Tasha blonde to Caro's dark. They dressed in similar fashion. Ready for anything, as in no tight skirts or ridiculously high heels like she'd been wearing the previous times their paths had crossed. However, she didn't appear to miss them much. He would admit that was part of the reason he had wanted her out here. To make her feel uncomfortable. While they hadn't been here very long, he wasn't sure his initial plan would work.

Jasmine Hoyer was full of surprises. Correction, Caro.

"Who is she to you?" Jimmy asked, leaning forward.

"Why?"

"Just curious."

He frowned recognizing the look of interest in Jimmy's expression. "Aren't you married with five kids?"

"No harm in looking."

Declan shook his head. He tolerated this man for Tasha's sake, no other reason. "Leave her alone, Jimmy. She's not for you."

"Is she yours?"

"If I say yes will you leave her alone?"

The man shrugged negligently.

"That's what I thought. Just, leave her alone." Declan wanted to scowl. Something else for him to tell her when they were alone.

"Tell me about her."

Why is he pushing this? "No. You will leave her alone, Jimmy. Don't think I'm kidding about this."

He held up his hands. "Fine. I won't chase her but if she comes to me..."

"You'll do nothing," Declan warned. "You're a married man with children." He closed his free hand into a fist. One he longed to punch Jimmy in the face with.

Jimmy gave his patented 'we'll see' smile and Declan grumbled under his breath. Moments later, feminine laughter filtered from the kitchen and he turned his head to see both women, heads bent together whispering and laughing.

I expected her to be a bitch this entire time and make my life a living hell. She's full of surprises. Getting along with Tasha. The dinner she made last night. His instincts were screaming that something was off and he swore he wouldn't let down his guard. Whatever Jasmine— Caro—was attempting wouldn't work. Her ass was staying here with him until they got the call to go back.

Caro's smile—as genuine as he'd ever seen it— struck a chord with him. *Really, Declan? You're getting soft on her? After all the hell she's put you through?* He didn't like the commentary from his brain and shoved it to the dark corners where he didn't have to listen.

"Declan?"

"What, Jimmy?" He tore his gaze from Caro and stared at the no account loser Tasha had wed.

"You ever regret getting divorced? Or is single life that much better?" The man's gaze drifted to Caro again.

He placed his mug down and leaned forward. "I'm not getting into this, Jimmy. You married her and the two of you have five children." *I could just kill him and bury him out here in the mountains. No one would find him. Tasha would be so much better off.*

"I get it, you don't want to share that piece of—"

"You should *really* stop talking." His words were more of a growl than anything.

Jimmy apparently heeded his warning, for nothing else spewed from his mouth. He stood abruptly then yelled, "Tasha, let's go."

Declan rose as the women parted. He disapproved of the looks on both their faces—they were disappointed. Caro said farewell but hung back, not going outside with them at all. He waved from the porch while they all piled into Jimmy's truck and drove away. As the tail lights vanished, he walked back inside the warm cabin.

Instantly the tension ratcheted up between him and the stunning woman standing opposite him in the kitchen. Purely sexual. Last night it had been hell for him to keep his hands off her. Never had lust affected him as it had since he'd gotten this woman on a plane.

She stared at him before understanding smoothed over her features and she rolled her eyes. "Don't worry. I know they won't help me." Caro rinsed her dishes then walked through the living room.

"Caro."

She stiffened but didn't turn. "What?"

"Keep away from Jimmy."

"Away from... Right, because I have no problem going after married men."

He crossed his arms, willing her to turn so he could stare at her face, not her back. "I'm not the one who propositioned Detective Lance Baldwin and when that failed made the same offer to his married partner." Lord, just speaking those words irritated him.

Her hands fisted before she whirled to face him. Flames lit her eyes as she glared at him. She was magnificent. When she approached him, alarm bells went off in his head. Hips swaying seductively, she licked her lips.

"What's the problem, McBride? Jealous because you weren't propositioned?" She approached closer.

His cock stiffened. He held her gaze, refusing to back down. "Is that what you're offering?"

A smile suited to a sex kitten turned up her lips, and he knew he was in trouble. This woman had somehow gotten complete power over him. The immunity he'd had to her before had vanished.

"Is that what you want? Me to walk closer, trail my fingers up your rock hard chest" — she did just that — "press against you and promise you anything you want?"

He groaned when she curved her fingers around his rigid cock and held him. Her lips were right there, tempting him with their lush fullness. Declan knew once he crossed this line there would be no going back.

He snapped an arm out, wrapping it around her shoulder, then sank his hand through the hair to grab the nape of her neck, before lifting her almost so their lips touched. She had to go up on her tiptoes, her breasts rubbed against him. Tantalizing. Provoking the need in him to rise to the top.

"Don't play with fire," he warned, teetering on the edge of his control.

Her gaze flicked from his eyes to his lips and back. Her breathing quickened and her pupils dilated as her nose flared slightly. She wanted him. Most likely as much as he wanted her.

"Scared to take what's being offered?"

Her breath, a mixture of sweetness and mint, flowed over him. He wanted her subtle scent all over him. And vice versa. He wanted her to smell like him. All over. From top to bottom he wanted to smell him on her.

He snapped his teeth close to her. "What would you do if I said I would take you up on it?" he asked, his voice a low thread of passion. "Would you stay where you are or run away and hide in your room? Would you let me take your clothes off until your body was naked beneath me? Let me lick you from head to foot, bury my face between your legs and eat your cream until you screamed my name as you came?"

He thought she would back off. He should have known better. Caro dragged her tongue along his lip. "Only if you let me suck on your big cock at the same time. I love to sixty-nine. You could eat all you want so long as you don't deny me the same pleasure."

It took him a minute to realize that the rumble had come from him. He flexed his hand on the nape of her neck and pressed his lips to hers. *Dear sweet Lord.* Soft, lush and perfect. He thrust his tongue in deep and she opened beneath him, no hesitation or anything. Her moan had his cock trying to punch free of his jeans.

Footsteps on the porch barely registered and he jerked away from her just as the door flew open. He whirled around to face the person.

"Dec— Oh, there you are." Martin took in the scene before him, one gray eyebrow rising. "Am I disturbing something?"

Hell yes. Behind him he heard her soft footfalls as she retreated. *Definitely disturbing something.*

"Nope. What's up, Martin?"

He jerked his hand over his shoulder. "I brought some more things for your...guest."

Declan moved toward his friend and mentor. "Things? I know you, Martin. What are you playing at?"

The men walked beyond the front door. Snow continued to fall and they passed through the deepening accumulation to get to Martin's SUV. Sure enough there were a few plastic bags in the back.

"I'm not playing at anything. You brought a woman here from the city. I know you didn't plan on fucking her the entire time. Although, maybe you did."

Declan's skin tingled at the thought. He cleared his throat and opened the door. "I'm not like that."

Martin placed a hand on his arm. "Listen to me, Declan McBride. I've known you since you were in diapers. Hell, longer than that. I knew your parents, you and my boy were brothers and when you lost your parents and I lost my son, we became family. You never brought that woman you married out here and I have never seen the emotions on your face like I do when I see you interacting with this Caro. From what you said about her before, I expected nothing but hatred between the two of you. What I see isn't hate. It's passion. Whatever that fine line between love and hate, the two of you are teetering on falling into the side you claim you don't want."

Declan grabbed most of the bags. "My wife wouldn't set foot here. I asked her once to go with me on a trip and she threw a fit that it wasn't going to be in a city. I never mentioned this place to her. No one knows about it, which is why I figured it would be safe for me to bring…Caro here."

Martin took the remaining bags. "So this is all about your job."

Even a deaf man would have picked up on the disbelief in Martin's tone. Declan shut the vehicle door.

"Yes."

"And had I not come when I did, where would you be right now?"

He blinked. Naked with Caro. "Inside." *Inside her.*

"I'm guessing you'd be in a room learning what it was like to live again and be with a woman." He chuckled. "I may be old, Declan, but I'm still a man and one who recognizes passion between two people. There was so much heat in your eyes when you faced me. I know where that was leading." He grinned. "There are some condoms in the bags as well."

"Condoms? You brought me condoms?" Christ why was it so hard to find his breath?

"Sure thing. Took them from the back so no one in town would know. You know business isn't all that private around here." Martin gazed around. "I know, I know. You're just protecting her. If both of you want it, why are you denying yourselves?"

"It's not proper."

"Son, there was a time when you and her in a house together *period* wouldn't be proper, not even with her sleeping in a room of her own. Times change. And I like her for you."

"You don't know what she's like."

"And maybe, for once in your life, you should forget what you read on paper about someone and look at her through fresh eyes. You'll always be a cop, Declan, but look around you. Where is she going to go? Even if she takes your vehicle, she doesn't know how to get out of here. Maybe all the bad you see is an act. Perhaps she's truly a nice person, one you actually could like. Not just fuck, although that is why I put condoms — and a lot of them — in the bag."

"I can't believe you're talking to me about this."

"Why is that? Because you don't want to face the truth? You're attracted to her? You don't have to be so unforgiving all the time, Declan. Enjoy being back here. Enjoy her. You don't have to be a cop all the time. You will still protect her even if you allow yourself to be human for a while."

Damn the old man for making sense.

Chapter Four

Her fingertips were cold. Caro left them upon the glass as she stared blindly past the bedroom window. *What the hell was I thinking? Did I really say those things to him?*

She had, and she dropped her head against the chilled glass in mortification. Something was seriously wrong with her. Those were not the actions of a sane woman. Not how she usually behaved.

I really need to read the file they have on me. Or rather on Jasmine. *When he said I went after married men, I snapped just like I did with the drug accusation. If I keep messing this up, he'll figure out I'm not really Jasmine and this whole ruse will be a bust.*

Those things he said, those accusations, weren't against her, but the twin she was doing this for. *I can't take his attacks so personally. He sees her when he looks at me, as he's supposed to, but I can't continue to expect him to judge me as Caro.*

She retreated from the window and sat on the bed, reaching for some more papers. Mindlessly she began to fold. A smile graced her lips when she thought about the reaction he'd had to her. One he couldn't hide.

That was for me, not Jasmine. Caro would be lying if she tried to pretend that Declan didn't arouse her. The man was just fucking hot. End of discussion.

Imagine what the days and nights would be like if you were to share a bed with him. Okay, so it wasn't like she hadn't already been thinking such things but still...

She sobered at the recollection of his last warning. To stay away from Jimmy. She shuddered. The man was a sleeze. It bothered her to no end that he would think of her in such a way while being married with five children. *Not like it doesn't bother me that Jasmine's past was such Declan thought I would be going after Jimmy just because.*

Caro rose from the bed, paper in hand, and walked to the door where she paused. What if Martin was still there? *What if he isn't?* Her breaths came quicker and she shook her head as she tried to regain some semblance of control.

"Declan?" she called out as she stepped from the room.

No one responded and she progressed farther. New wood had been brought in and set by the fireplace. The cabin wasn't all that big, it was cozy. Intimate. Hard for him to not be seen if he was present.

Unless he's in his bedroom. She turned her head and glanced over her shoulder to the closed door. Worrying her lower lip, she debated knocking on the door. *That may not be the smartest thing I've done.*

Nope. Instead she headed for the living room. A shadow moved by one window and she peered out. There were no vehicles in the yard so Martin must have departed. The door opened and in walked Declan with another armful of wood.

His gaze scorched her as he neared, bypassed her then placed the wood down. She'd been unable to move, just stared at him.

"Need some help?" she offered.

His attention flickered between her lips and eyes before he gave a brief nod. "Sure. Fill up the box here and place some on the side. I'll move some more from the shed to the house."

She slid the partially done crane in her pocket. "You think it's going to get colder tonight?"

"I think from this snow it's going to dump on us. I don't want to have to go out in a blizzard if that's what comes." He whirled about and strode to the door.

Caro stared unabashedly at his ass. *Damn those jeans looked good on him.* He didn't wear a jacket, so the flannel shirt tucked into well-fitting jeans allowed her to ogle. Shaking herself from the daze, she shoved her feet into her hiking boots and followed him outside. She pulled the door behind her but didn't shut it all the way.

She took a few trips herself until the box inside had been filled to the top. The physical exercise felt good so she went back out, this time fully shutting the door, and trudged through the accumulated snow to the shed where he looked up from getting another load.

"Where's your jacket?"

She narrowed her eyes. "Where's yours?"

"I wasn't shot. Go back inside."

"My head is covered," she said tugging on one side of her knit cap. "The injury is covered if that's what the concern is. I don't know why you—" She took a ragged breath, the scent of him mingling with that of the wood and the crisp outdoors. "I don't want to fight. I came to help."

He assessed her for a few moments then shrugged as if he didn't have a single care in the world. "Fine."

Declan walked off. She loaded up her own arms and made the trek to the porch. They lined both sides of the door before he called it quits. He held the door and gestured for her to go in first.

Caro wanted to stay out and enjoy the cold a bit more. It was the perfect temperature and she longed to explore. Not wanting to be inside at the moment, she reached up for her jacket and slipped it on.

"What are you doing?" he asked, closing the door behind him.

"I wanted to go outside and walk around. Explore a bit."

His jaw flexed a few times and he rolled those massive shoulders of his before blowing out a breath.

"There are no houses within a short distance of here. Stay within yelling distance of the cabin. Be mindful of bears. If there are some who've yet to go into hibernation you don't want to stumble onto them."

Okay, so he wanted to scare her. "I won't go far."

Declan swung the door open and closed it behind her. As she strode down the step and into the snow she knew he watched her. Caro didn't turn just kept going. The fresh air uplifted her and she smiled as her entire body relaxed. This she could handle. More snow fell as she continued her mindless walking.

When she headed back, she'd been out for two hours. The cabin came into view as she walked across a meadow. Smoke churned from the chimney and she gave a small grin. *Like a postcard or a Christmas card picture.*

She knocked the snow off her boots as best she could on the porch then entered. The warmth seeped into her like she'd just drunk some fine cognac. One of her favorite parts of being out on a cold day, coming inside and warming up. Now all she needed was a cup of hot cocoa, with marshmallows, and she'd be in heaven.

"Have fun?" Declan's baritone wove around her and made her warm for an entirely different reason. *Warm? More like hot.*

"I did, thank you." She unzipped and slid off her jacket before hanging it on the peg. Her hat followed then she bent down to undo her boots. "Is all of this yours?"

"Yes. I don't think you walked far enough to get off my property."

Damn. Pulling her feet free, she rubbed her head, unpleased with the ache that seemed to want to persist in lingering.

"Headache?"

"I'm fine," she said, putting her boots against the wall.

She walked to the coffee maker and shook her head. Nope, she wanted hot chocolate. If she just knew where he'd put it.

"What are you looking for?" His voice was closer now.

She opened a cupboard. "Hot chocolate."

He got it down for her and stepped back. "Martin brought you some games and books — he thought you might get bored here with me."

"I'll make sure to thank him when I see him again."

She filled the kettle, enough for two just in case, and placed it on the stove. Glancing at the container of cocoa, she smiled at the sight of a bag of marshmallows beside it. Declan sat at the table, long legs out before him as he looked at her.

"Do you have my file?" she asked with her back to him, rooting around in a drawer for a spoon.

"Why?"

"Just wanted to read what you had on me. That's all."

She turned in time to see him push to his feet with a singularly fluid movement. Declan left the room and she blew out a breath. There went a lot of man. She turned off the burner when the kettle whistled. Adding the water to the mix, she stirred it slowly then plopped in a few marshmallows.

Outside, the wind increased in speed and swirled the falling snow around. *Only to me would this happen. A picture perfect scene. Mountains, snow, a warm fire burning in a small cabin and a hot ass man—which will culminate in my fingering myself to release tonight in bed. Why? Because this man thinks I'm my twin and can't stand me. All the while I'm yearning for something so simple as a touch. A simple brush of skin, the feel of his hard body behind mine, pressing into me.*

"Here."

His voice surprised her and she jumped. He held out a tablet for her and she reached for it. Ensuring their fingers didn't touch, she took it from him and made her way to the table. He had it all there for her to look at and she sat before beginning to read.

The first part she read was about the family she was to be witness against. The Kazakova crime family. Each line Caro read soured her gut even more. *Shit, how did I get caught up in this?* The lengthy list of murders they blamed the family for but couldn't ever prove because of lack of witnesses and questionable circumstantial evidence. How they tortured people. Again, no witnesses.

Look at me, a quiet girl, good from all accounts. Now I'm caught up in a lie so deep I don't know if I'll ever climb out. Not to mention I'm now going up against a crime syndicate which will most likely kill me. She turned the pages and kept reading. *Or my family and friends.*

God, she had to get free of here. After all that interesting and life sucking information she'd discovered on the Kazakova family, she found Jasmine's rap sheet.

Holy shit, Jasmine. You're a terror.

Declan started the coffee machine, needing to occupy his time. She didn't sit with her back to him so he utilized the opportunity to observe her as she read the information on the tablet. It bothered her, that much he could tell. Her jaw clenched occasionally and her fingers tightened around the mug.

Wonder if she's laughing about missing stuff that we don't know about?

She didn't look at all amused, actually. Quite the opposite.

Her hair, not that hideous shade of pink it had been previously, fell in soft waves around her face. She kept it tucked behind her ear and he noted, with a bit of surprise, she only wore simple gold studs. Nothing outlandish or dangling as she had worn previously. *It's like she's a whole other person.*

He poured his coffee and fixed it the way he liked it before resting against the counter and just outright staring at her. The simple gray sweatshirt and blue jeans made her look soft. Approachable.

Sexy, don't forget sexy.

As if he could. Hell, his cock was still hard from their earlier interaction. He couldn't get it out of his mind.

Some cop I am. Martin's words came back to him and he thought about it. Why should he bother denying the attraction between the two of them? They were both adults and, so long as it was consenting on both ends, whose business was it what they did? It's not like his position intimidated her. That had been proven numerous times during prior confrontations.

His CB radio crackled, bringing her head up as Martin's voice came through.

"Declan. Pick up if you're able."

He walked to the other side of the small yet open kitchen and lifted the handset. "What's up, Martin?"

"You have someone who called looking for you. Jackie."

He groaned and set his coffee cup down. "I'll be right down." He left his drink and went to build up the fire so it would be warm there when they came back.

"Let's go," he said heading to the door and grabbing his coat from the peg.

She obviously wasn't in as much of a rush for she finished her drink, rinsed it out then left the mug in the sink. He departed the cabin as she sat on the bench and tied on her hiking boots.

He had the Jeep by the cabin when she stepped out on the porch. With eyebrows nearly raised to the edge of her black and white knit cap she held up his tablet. Declan shook his head and she vanished briefly before closing the distance to the vehicle.

Once she'd buckled herself in, he got going. The large tires cut easily through the snow as he moved from the drive and put them on the road. Martin's tracks were not readily recognizable anymore. Caro leaned against the door and remained silent. If she was checking and making notes on how to get to town, well, he would start removing the distributor cap until he needed to use the Jeep. That would eliminate her taking the vehicle.

He parked along the plowed main drag and killed the engine. They both hopped out of his vehicle. The street sat empty with no signs of life. He knew where people were. In the warmth of Ted's Diner.

Declan gazed over the hood at Caro. She had her head tipped back, eyes closed as the flakes fell and settled gently upon her. It dotted her cap, skin and jacket.

She appeared so peaceful.

"Come on."

He saw it then. The transformation. Her entire body stiffened and her features hardened.

"Might help," she snapped, "if I knew where I was supposed to go. I wouldn't have to keep you waiting." She stared at him, condemnation lighting her face. "Not to mention I'm not a dog to jump at your every command. You could have left me at the cabin."

True, he could have. Why he had made her come with him, he hadn't any idea. "Go to Ted's Diner and get something to eat. I'll be there shortly."

She glared at him before striking off across the street. Declan waited until she had stepped inside the diner before he took himself to Martin's. The man gave him a small nod as he spied him.

"Thanks for the call, Martin."

"She sounds just as lovely as you made her out to be. I'm glad you never brought her to this place."

"Me too." Declan picked up the phone that he knew she wouldn't be able to trace and called her back.

"Jacquelyn Ashcraft's office."

He didn't recognize the voice of the woman who answered. It didn't surprise him—Jackie didn't keep people around a long time. She was a hard woman to work for. Hard to live with and stay married to as well.

"I need to speak with Ms Ashcraft. I'm returning her call."

"Who may I say is calling, please?"

"Declan McBride."

"One moment, Mr McBride." She placed him on hold.

He paced while waiting.

"Where the hell are you, McBride?" Jacquelyn barked seconds later.

He rolled his eyes. "Doing what I said I would do. Protecting your witness."

"Where?"

"See, funny thing, ADA Ashcraft, I'm not telling you. No one knows, that's why it's a safe place for her to be."

"Come on, Declan." Her voice turned soft and seductive. "Let me know. I'm the prosecutor for crying out loud. I need to know she's safe."

He cracked his neck, strolled to the nearest window then peered out. "She is. You'll just have to take my word on that."

"I can force you to tell," she snarled, not a single trace of the seduction from before.

"Really? How are you going to do that?" He didn't like being pushed.

"I will call your boss."

"Call my LT. He doesn't know where I am either. But let me make this perfectly clear. The next time you call here, Jackie, had better be to tell me she's needed back in court. Or I won't be calling you back."

Caro walked by up the street and he frowned. *I thought I told her to go into the diner.* She wasn't running but strolling as if she had all the time in the world.

"You make me lose this case, Declan…"

He chuckled over the warning in her tone. "You don't scare me, Jackie. I know you do many others there. But not me. Remember I was married to you."

"Don't remind me," she bit off.

"Then I suggest you don't forget I'm damn good at my job and I don't do well with being strong-armed. Your witness will be fine and I'll have her there for court. Like I said, give me forty-eight hours' notice."

Jackie launched another litany of something but he ended the call and handed the phone to Martin who'd moved to stand beside him.

"Not pleased?"

Declan laughed. "Jackie's never been pleased. She doesn't know the meaning of the word."

"What was it about her that had you marry her?"

He shook his head. "I was younger and foolish. Thought I was in love." Declan walked toward the door. "When I didn't go for detective she got pissed because I wasn't ambitious enough and she couldn't be married to a regular cop. How would that look, a woman going for the DA's spot married to a beat cop? Not in her grand scheme."

"Bitch," Martin groused.

"You don't know the half of it." He smacked him on the shoulder. "Thanks for alerting me to the call. I have to go see where Caro is going. Then get back to the cabin before more snow falls."

"Drive safe. I put some more stuff in your Jeep while you were on the phone. Can't have you running out of food now."

Declan didn't see that happening. "We'll be fine, Martin."

"Take care of her, Declan. She's something else."

Another snort. "Don't I know it."

Martin grabbed his hand and halted him. "I mean something special, Declan."

Of course he did. Declan just smiled and strode outside with a wave over one shoulder. Turning his head, he tried to see the woman he was after. No one was in view. With a muttered grumble, he jogged across the street and off in the direction he'd seen her.

He located her in the small park in town. She sat on a bench, back to him, facing the small lake. Shoving his hands in his pockets, he moved up behind her.

"What are you doing here?" he asked.

She didn't even turn around. "Thinking."

Declan went around the bench and lowered himself to the seat beside her. He stretched out his legs and sighed heavily. "About?" He stared at her hand, which lay on her lap. She constantly moved her fingers.

She tipped her head and glanced at him. "Is this an interrogation, Officer?"

"Consider it more like an olive branch."

Chapter Five

The odds weren't very high in her favor and Caro frowned. *At least I don't think so.* She snuck another peek at her cards then at the growing pile of chocolate and candy in the middle of the table. Lifting her gaze, she found Declan staring at her. Endless patience and no other expression.

Poker. This was not her game. He was teaching her. Sort of. More like he was kicking her ass.

The stint in town had gone pretty well. They'd just sat and talked about a few things while enjoying the park. It had been an olive branch and she had decided to be nicer to him, no matter what the crap listed in her twin's file said. And there was a lot there but she figured that with as much lying as Jasmine did, being nice at a point would be acceptable. She'd do whatever it took to get the desired results. He may not believe it but this way she could live with herself better. The lying already ate at her.

"Well?" he asked. His firm lips had a slight tilt to them, showing his amusement.

"I'm thinking."

He held up a hand as if to say 'okay, sorry' and reclined back in his chair. The lights were low around them, creating a bit of an intimate atmosphere. Before him, a beer sat on the table and an identical one sat in front of her as well. A large bowl of chips — potato — sat between them slightly off to the side.

Caro couldn't remember if he'd said a straight beat a flush or not. The full boat — or house — beat something else and... Yeah, she was most assuredly and definitely confused. *Not telling him that, though.*

"I raise." She slid in the higher 'chips' to join the rest of the collection in the center.

He sat forward and lifted his heavily lashed eyes until his blue eyes held hers. "You sure you want to do that?"

No. I would be much more confident if we played chess. "Absolutely," she said with confidence she unquestionably didn't feel.

Declan didn't even peek at his cards, and the wolfish grin that lifted his lips released waves of uncertainty within her.

He knows something about what I have.

"I call."

Had any two words ever sounded so sexual to her before? *Maybe the better question would be — should be — why I'm thinking about sex. Oh yeah, that's right. The reaction I have at the deep stroke of his voice. The way his heated gaze makes me want to squirm on the chair. Or was that rip off my shirt and bra to see what he'd do? Both? More?*

"You call." She sniffed. "What kind of poker is this again?"

He took a swig of his beer, the movement of his throat sidetracking her as his Adam's apple rolled up and down. Declan held her gaze, heat surging through his eyes. "Stud poker. And yes, I call."

Her pussy creamed and she did her best to not show how his words and voice affected her. *Why did his words sound like a promise? And why is that turning me on even more?*

"Okay..." She reached out for a potato chip and ate it. "Do I have to raise now?"

His head shake was lazy. "You can or not. You could also fold."

Fold? No way. "Give up? I don't think so." She stared at his pile. He had more than she did and it wouldn't pay to be reckless.

"What's it going to be?"

She licked her lips and lifted her chin before grabbing for her bottle. "Show me."

This time his smile was pure sin. "Love to."

He began flipping his cards over and she stared. Not at his cards, no, she locked onto his hand. Strong. Scarred. Masculine. Long fingers and clean square nails.

"Your turn."

Damn man and his voice were lethal. She turned hers over. "I believe I have a flush."

He shook his head and whistled low. "Not just a flush."

She looked down at her cards again. It hit her after a few more glances. "A straight flush."

"This hand's yours."

Caro stared at his. Two pair, ace high. No wonder he had been cocky. She didn't even bother hiding her grin as she scooped the pile toward her. He reached over and took her cards before shuffling them while she made neat little piles out of her candy. Wouldn't do to get them mixed up and have her even more confused on what was what.

"What are you thinking?" he asked.

"Huh?" She stared at him. "What am I thinking about what?"

"Just now. You had this quirk of a smile on your face. What were you thinking?"

She ducked her head as the blush skated along her cheeks. "Just that I needed to make all neat piles. And how I want to eat one of those gold ones."

His grin was raw sex. "So eat one."

"They're the highest amount and if I take one then I don't have as much."

He reached from his stack of them—his much larger one—and flipped her two. "There you go. Enjoy."

She palmed them only to pause. "Why would you give me two?"

"I enjoy watching a woman eat something she's craving." One shoulder lifted languidly. "Some women, that is."

Lord help her, if she were straddling his leg she would be humping him like a dog. There it went again, that tilt of his lips. She knew he was baiting her and she didn't care. If this night ended up with her in his bed, she had no problem with that. Caro unwrapped one, placed the second to her left, where it wasn't in her organized piles, and popped the chocolate in her mouth.

A moan slid free as the silky goodness coated her tongue. He jerked back, his chair skidding along the wood floor. She met his gaze and lifted an eyebrow. Declan coughed and got up to walk to the kitchen. She watched him move, mesmerized by his ass and the way his jeans cupped it. *I'd like to cup it. Sink my nails into it as he's between my legs and thrusts his cock in and out of me. Wrap my legs around his waist and draw him in as tight as I could. As deep as possible.*

He froze and gripped the edge of the counter. She shook herself free of the sexual haze surrounding her and focused on the table.

"What's that?" he asked when he returned to his seat.

"What's what?"

"That. In your hand. Gold."

It took her a moment to realize she'd made a crane. "Crane."

She put it in the palm of her hand and stretched it out to him. Even though his fingers didn't touch her when he took it from her, she swore she felt him. Perhaps it was just her overactive imagination but in her mind, she experienced the heat of his fingertips sliding along her hypersensitive skin.

The light brush of calluses. The coiled strength she knew he had in his touch. *I have* got *to get a hold of myself.*

He inspected it closely and nodded as he placed it down by his side. "Nice."

Okay, so I guess he's keeping it. He picked up the deck and shuffled a bit more.

"Ready?" he asked.

She was ready for something… Caro nodded, not trusting her voice.

Two hands later she had nothing but the gold chocolates before her. She bemoaned her lack of luck and Declan grinned as he shuffled.

"Not funny," she griped.

"Depends on the seat you're in."

"I thought I was supposed to learn."

"You are. You're learning that if you don't play smart you will lose."

She grunted and reached for the other piece of chocolate he'd tossed her earlier to eat. Popping it in her mouth, she watched him from below lowered lashes as his eyes followed every movement. She released a low groan of pleasure and noticed how his eyes darkened and he shifted in his seat.

"I'm learning all right," she admitted.

Caro touched her index finger to the corner of her mouth, making sure there was no chocolate residing there. Again, he followed the motion. *Oh yes, I'm learning.*

She had no more beer to drink so she rose to get some water, making sure to take her time as she tried to figure out what to do. Her body was primed and needed some release. Soon. Preferably by someone other than herself.

Get a hold of yourself, Caro, she reprimanded herself. *He's got you here to keep you safe, not because you are the woman he wants in his bed. Although, that exchange this morning could have changed his mind.*

"Coming?"

Damn near to it. She filled the glass and made her way back to the table. She made another crane from the remaining free sheet of gold wrapping and placed it to her left. Caro sucked the tip of her pinky as she waited for him to deal. He just sat there, gaze riveted to her.

"Remember what I said about playing with fire?" His voice, low and gravelly, stroked places no man had touched for a long time. *Too damn long.*

She held his stare, dragged her tongue along her lower lip before putting the little finger back in. "I haven't. Make sure you don't forget what I said either." Caro stood and reached over to the pile he had and stole a bunch of his loot. In the middle of the table she created the numbers sixty-nine. "Says the same thing no matter how you look at it." Her words were soft.

His chair hit the floor as he shot to his feet. Lust rocked her and she didn't move as he was suddenly at her side. Declan hauled her up and slammed his mouth over hers. Instantly, she melted into his hard chest, gripping him, digging her fingers into the rock hard triceps beneath them. His taste surged into her mouth, mixing perfectly with the chocolate she'd just finished.

He'd lost his mind. His sanity. His capability for sensible thought. All he knew was Caro. The press of her soft body against his hard one. The sweet taste of her. The added chocolate and how it hardened his cock as their tongues danced with one another.

Kicking the chair out of the way, Declan turned them and laid her back on the table. He deepened the kiss as his body pressed against her softer one. This had to be the stupidest thing he could do but there was no more stopping the lust that pumped freely through him. She widened her legs, cradling the ridge of his hard cock between her legs, where he longed to be, only in his version they were without any clothing between them.

He ground against her, reveling in the whimper that escaped from her slender throat. Her shudder preceded her grabbing at his shoulders and digging into him with strong fingers.

"Declan."

Lord, her voice, deep and sexy, skated like flames along his skin.

"Jas—"

"Caro," she interrupted. "Call me Caro."

He'd call her whatever she wanted. "Caro it is," he rumbled before claiming her mouth in another near bruising kiss. Their teeth clashed as they battled for dominance. He couldn't get enough.

When her fingers went for his button, he didn't stop her, just attacked her pants. It didn't take long before she lay on his kitchen table naked. She held his gaze without fear or hesitation as she reached a hand out and curved it around his hard dick. She swiped her thumb over the head, smearing the pre-cum. He groaned low in his throat and spun her around so that her head hung over the edge. There would be time later to learn her body and take pleasure in memorizing every inch. Right now, there was something else on his mind.

Her pussy lips gleamed in the soft lighting and the moisture on them gave away her own heightened desire. Bending down, hands braced on her hips and ass, he spread her lips as her mouth covered his cock. *Fuck me!*

He sank his tongue into her slit and began to lap as she moved her head up and down combined with the soft touch of her hand. She readjusted, widening her legs to make it easier for him and he took advantage. She tasted...perfect. A heady mixture of things he could never begin to explain and a taste he never wanted to lose. Her thick cream coated his tongue as she took him in deep.

He sucked on her clit, sliding two fingers inside her hot pussy. She shifted against him, working her hips to bring him in deeper. Declan didn't know how much longer he was going to be able to keep this up. His legs didn't want to hold him given the way her mouth worked his shaft.

Declan closed his eyes at the light caress of her fingertips along his balls as she continued to suck him. He withdrew his fingers and plunged his tongue in her as he cupped her thigh. She continued to grind against him as he lapped, stabbed, and licked her. Her body stiffened seconds before she arched and came with a rush around his tongue.

The vibration from her cry reverberated up his shaft and he knew he was gone as well. He shot deep into her throat, ropes of his cum. She purred and took it all. When he was done, he backed out of her mouth carefully and stood staring down at her naked body.

She shifted beneath his gaze and the light reflected off the candy that had stuck to the outside of her leg. Declan ran a slow perusal of her form. Curves. Dips. Swells. A woman. Not a stick. But a true woman. She had curves that would put Marilyn Monroe to shame.

Caro dragged her tongue over her lips as if she sought more of him. More of his taste. She didn't move, didn't try to hide her body from him nor did she shy away from staring at him. His cock continually drew her attention. In the depths of her brown eyes he could read her hunger. She wanted more.

Good. So did he.

He walked around the table, allowing her to remain there, sprawled as she was amongst the shiny candy wrappers and discarded cards. Declan stepped between her legs and drew her flush until her wet pussy cradled his cock. She watched him, her thick curved lashes giving her a hooded sensual appearance. Her hair pillowed her head. Full breasts with tightly drawn nipples begged attention as did her flat belly and waxed pussy.

He worked his hips, allowing his cock to glide along her wetness, and he leaned to capture her breasts. He lifted their weight and watched her eyes darken with increased pleasure. Every inch of her was highly sensitive and responsive. He loved that.

Teasing her nipples with his thumbs, he grinned wickedly with the responding flush of her skin and increased breathing. He plucked at her until she squirmed against his rigid shaft.

"Declan."

"I want to fuck you." He bent down and sucked on her nipple. "Repeatedly" — he drew on the other one — "on every surface available to us."

She sank a hand into his hair, holding him against her. "Yes."

Her affirmation was more of a whisper than anything but he heard it like it had been shot out of a cannon. Caro dug her left heel into his ass cheek, encouraging him closer. It would be so simple for him to slide inside her, to feel the velvet walls ripple around his bare cock.

Condom.

"One second," he rasped, stepping away.

He grabbed a condom from his bedroom then strode back to find her still sprawled on the table. An offering to him. One difference, she had one hand pushing a piece of chocolate into her mouth while the other...dallied in her pussy.

"Fuck," he said. Ripping open the condom packet, he stared at her plunging fingers. Declan rolled on the protection and stepped back between her thighs. She sucked on her index finger.

He grasped his cock while he used his other hand to remove her fingers from her slickness. Her smell surrounded him and he guided them to his mouth where he licked them clean of her essence.

As he pressed his cock into her, he kissed her. Their combined tastes filled his senses. Her moan accompanied the thrust of her tongue along his.

Christ, her pussy held him so perfectly.

"Hot. Wet. Tight." He never wanted to leave.

She bucked against him then hooked her legs tight around his waist. "Oh God, Declan… Move."

He did.

Chapter Six

Caro whimpered and rolled her hips as she leaned forward, resting her palms on Declan's muscled torso. He sat buried balls deep within her heated pussy, yet she still ground against him more. The mattress beneath her feet moved with them. They'd finally made it to his bedroom.

The intensity of her craving should have scared her. Perhaps it would…later. The here and now belonged to her and the man fucking her brains out.

He gripped her waist, undulating beneath her, working in perfect tandem with her own strokes, heightening every second of pleasured bliss. Up and down she rose and fell on his hard shaft. Their sweat-soaked skin slid along one another as they moved.

She came with a keening cry, back bowing as her world splintered around her into a rainbow of sparks. His roar echoed around her moments later.

Caro sank forward and lay utterly spent and exhausted upon his chest. He wrapped his strong arms around her and held her close. And tight. She didn't mind.

Odd, considering I usually hate cuddling after sex. This session had gone on for hours. Tender and slow. Rough and fast. What had started in the kitchen had gone through the small cabin. Furniture, counters, floor, it didn't matter. Even the walls had gotten in on it. Muscles she never even knew existed in her body ached. *So worth it, though.*

"I need to check the fire." His words rumbled along her skin.

"So I need to move?" Seriously? She didn't think she had the energy.

"We can go this way but it's your ass that's by the fire." He trailed his fingers along her spine. "I like being buried inside your tight pussy."

Yeah, she was beginning to see that for herself. She slowly maneuvered off him. "I'd prefer not to have sparks on my ass, thanks."

He disposed of the condom and paused to grab a pair of sweats from his dresser. She readjusted and lay on her side, holding the pillow he'd been on as she watched him hide his tanned skin from her gaze.

His blue-green stare burned her and set her body aflame once more. Hungrily, she took in what he offered—the visual feast for her eyes.

He had swiftly and succinctly removed all her inhibitions with a single touch. No, she'd not been a prude—not in her mind—but she had never been so unashamed with her body as she had just been these past few hours with Declan McBride.

Declan winked then strode from the room, leaving her alone with her streaming thoughts. She debated on getting up from his ridiculously comfortable bed and cleaning up but she refrained. There was something to be said about smelling like the man who had just rocked your world. So she grinned and burrowed deeper beneath the blankets.

Lord, he wore me out. She blinked and watched him return to the bedroom. He latched onto her gaze and sent her another wink.

"All set for the night."

Wonder if that means I should leave to the other bed?

Before she could ask, he kicked off his sweats and climbed in beside her, drawing her back into the warm circle of his embrace. Caro didn't fight, she yawned and pressed against him tighter.

"Keep rubbing against me like that and you won't be getting any sleep."

"Really?" *Lordy, there was way too much hope in my voice there.* "I can sleep tomorrow," she said, lifting one of his hands and guiding it to between her pussy lips, moaning again at the feel of his touch.

* * * *

Caro stirred and opened her eyes. Muted sunlight poured through the glass highlighting the snow outside as well as the fact it was late afternoon. *Did I really sleep so long?* She sat up, holding the top blanket against her bare, slightly abraded breasts. The bedroom was empty. Aside from her, of course. The propped open door didn't allow any sounds to filter back to her.

Where is he?

The unease from mornings after—why she didn't stay nights—sank in. *Maybe he just wants me to leave.* She rose from the bed, her clothes nowhere to be found. Borrowing his blanket, she wrapped it around her nude form and padded to the door where she slipped through and went to the bedroom he'd given her. Her stuff was there and she took a quick shower before dressing.

He had the cabin warm enough so she didn't mind having her hair damp. She retreated to his room again and proceeded to make his bed, running her hands over the pillow cases as she fixed them.

The pass of his work-roughened hands along her sensitive skin.

She blinked and gulped before tugging up the blankets.

His heavy weight bearing her back into the mattress as his thick cock thrust deep.

She exhaled sharply and spread the final covering back over his bed. Bending over to tuck it in, she gave a wry grin at the sight of another condom wrapper. She picked it up and tossed it in the trash.

His stubble-covered jaw abrading her inner thighs as he lapped at her pussy with endless licks.

Her legs shook and she tried hard to shove those images from her mind. They were so raw and powerful it was like a replay she actually experienced on her skin. "Fuck," she muttered as she finished making his bed.

Turning around she drew up short at the sight of him leaning in the doorway. Unease filled her. She clasped her hands before her and gave him a shy smile. He stared at her until she wanted to hide. She couldn't read his expression.

"Sleep well?" His voice was deep and raspy.

"Yes, thank you. Did you?"

He pushed away from the frame and approached her with a fluid motion. "Best I have in a long time."

What am I supposed to say to that? "Why didn't you wake me?"

Heat surged into that amazing gaze. "You looked exhausted."

She had been. But he had been up as long as she had. He paused before her, wrapped his hand in her wet hair and tugged it back.

"Don't think I wasn't, for I was. I just had some things to take care of and I didn't think you needed to be up for me doing them. You sleep well during the day and we can stay up late" — his lips brushed the corner of her mouth — "and see what happens."

Her heart beat out a tattoo in her chest. "Sounds good to me. Are you napping?"

"Didn't you just get out of bed?"

She held his gaze. "I meant for you."

"I wouldn't want to nap alone."

There wasn't any way she could ignore what he meant by that. Her stomach growled and she shrugged. "Sorry, I have to feed this complaining thing so I'll do that then make dinner."

He held her stare before he nodded. "Keep your strength up." Another teasing kiss before he backed off.

Caro left and walked to the kitchen. She started making dinner and while it sat in the oven, she ate a single piece of bread with peanut butter. That would tide her over until their meal was ready.

The knock at the door shocked her and she jumped. *I can't believe how fearful I am here. I should be safe, that's why he brought me here.*

Didn't stop her from letting him answer the door, however, and she didn't fail to notice the butt of his sidearm sticking up from the back of his waistband. He swung the door wide to admit Tasha.

"Hi, Declan," she said with a smile. "Are you sure I'm not intruding?"

"Not at all. You two have fun, I have some things to do out in the shed." Declan looked over his shoulder and Caro's breath hitched at the heat she witnessed in his eyes as he looked her over from head to toe. Then it changed and she saw him giving her a pointed look that she knew to mean she had better behave. All emotion was wiped away and in its place was what she referred to as his 'cop expression', all seriousness. He swiped his jacket and walked out.

Caro finished the last bite of her bread and stood. "Hi, Tasha."

"Are you sure you're not busy and are up for some company?"

"Please, he's not all that talkative. I would love some. Where are the children?"

"Staying with some friends. Jimmy is…out at one of his whore's houses."

Caro knew her eyes had grown wide. "I'm sorry?"

A shrug. "I know he cheats on me. I just don't have the means yet to get away. I'm working on it but not there." A forced smile. "I didn't come to depress you. I came to talk and have some fun."

"Coffee or hot chocolate?" Caro asked as she walked to the counter.

"Coffee and cookies."

A sound had her turning around.

Tasha set a large container on the table. "I brought the cookies."

A smile curved up Caro's lips. "Wonderful." Once the coffee had begun to percolate, Caro returned to the table with two plates and sat across from her visitor. "So, tell me what you know about Declan McBride."

Tasha's answering grin filled her face. She bit into the chocolate chip cookie and glanced around as if expecting the man himself to jump out and stop her. "The stories I have about Declan. Let me tell you."

* * * *

Declan finished changing the oil in his Jeep, and as he wiped his hands on a rag, he stared back at the cabin. Smoke continued to churn from the chimney and he knew the fire was doing fine. Caro. Jasmine. It didn't matter what she called herself, that woman had rocked his world every night since they'd first given in to the lust that poured between them fast, hot and strong. *And this morning...*

He chuckled at his brain's commentary. He hooked his ankles and continued to watch the log cabin. She had fitted in much better than he'd expected her to. Yes, he was still suspicious.

Caro took daily walks but she never once complained about being away from the hustle and bustle Atlanta brought to those who lived there. No more gaudy clothing or sickly perfumes. None of what he'd associated with Jasmine.

"Perhaps she's trying to be this Caro person."

None of his suspicion mattered when they got together on an intimate level, though. Then it wasn't him being a cop and her a witness. It was nothing more than one man and one woman. Him and her. And the exploding passion between them.

Tasha had come over a few times, which didn't bother him. The times that Jimmy came, he was much more careful not to leave the women alone with him. One day Jimmy had arrived on his own and Declan had been ready to yell at her but Caro had spent Jimmy's entire visit in her bedroom, not even coming out to interact with him past a hello and farewell.

He slammed the hood on his Jeep and tossed the rag onto the small table before he drew his gloves back on and left, pausing to shut the door. The snow had stopped for the day but he knew more was on the way. "Bet by tonight it's snowing again."

Declan was making his way back to the cabin when he spied her tracks heading off into the woods. *I must have been under the Jeep when she left because I didn't hear or see her.* Without thought, he altered his trajectory and tracked her.

Coming upon her, he slowed and stared at the woman who sat on a rock, one foot dangling over the edge. She'd had to climb up from the other side to make it there. From all appearances, Caro was lost in thought. Her arms were latched around her other leg and her chin rested upon her knee.

The corner of her mouth turned down slightly. He noticed tear tracks down one cheek. They'd been here for a week and while for him it was coming home, he understood why she didn't quite feel the same. He broke from the tree line and made his way to her. As he paused next to her, she turned her head and stared at him.

"You need something?"

He angled his head and moved so the sun wasn't in his eyes. "Do you?"

"No. Any idea how much longer this is going to be?"

Irritation pricked him. She couldn't be bothered to remain here? "Something else you have to do?"

He knew she wanted to say something but she merely shook her head. "Just wondering."

"I will put in a call tomorrow when I go to town and get some more supplies. Find out if they have a court date."

"Okay," she said. Caro took a deep breath and drew her other leg up.

"How long have you been out here?"

"Not sure. Why?"

"Come on, let's go inside."

She turned and stared between his face and his outstretched hand. She took it and he assisted her off the rock. "Okay, just one thing first." Caro pulled free.

"What's that?"

Smack! She tossed a handful of snow in his face then took off running, laughter trailing behind her. He wiped the wetness off and tracked her movement across the meadow. *I asked for that. I truly did.*

"Better keep running, Caro!" he called seconds before he charged off after her.

He overtook her without much effort and tackled her to the ground. Her squeal had him grinning as he returned the favor of putting snow in her face.

"What happened to protecting and serving?" she sputtered as he rolled them over on the snowy ground and stared into her eyes.

"I'm doing it."

She shook her head. "How so?"

"I'm protecting myself by getting you back and serving my need for revenge."

"I don't think that's what they meant by that saying."

"It's all in the interpretation, sexy."

"More like manipulation of the words."

"Depends on which side you're on."

"Mine," she said with a slight elevation in her tone.

He laughed again and kissed her swiftly before rising off her and helping her back to her feet. Staring down at her, he couldn't help but notice how the sparkle had returned to her gaze. This was what he wanted for her.

What the hell am I thinking? She's not mine. She's a fucking witness to a case. I just have to keep her safe then deliver her back in time. The thoughts chilled him in a way the snowy outdoors never could. He drew back and gestured for her to lead the way to the cabin. Right now, he didn't need her assessing and soft gaze upon him. Sex was one thing but getting emotionally involved was another kettle of fish. *One I don't need to open.*

Once they got closer to the cabin he noticed a vehicle waiting there. From her muttered curse, he realized Caro recognized the driver around the same moment he did. Jimmy.

Her steps slowed and he cut his gaze to the side. She smoothed away the frown and put an emotionless smile in its place. She shut down. Declan wasn't sure what to make of that. He'd thought she would have wanted to hit Jimmy up for some recreational sex.

You're just jealous at the thought of her wanting to be in bed with another man, his brain commented to him and he wasn't at all in the mood to listen. Not at all. Regardless if it was the truth or not.

Jimmy leaned against the side of the cabin when they approached and Declan strode ahead, wanting to keep this man away from her. The desire didn't come from the part of him that was cop, no, it was pure proprietary need. Caveman attitude and alpha male. Hell, were he a dog he'd think about pissing in a circle around her so the man would possibly get the hint to leave his woman fucking alone. *Yeah, I said it. My woman.* He wasn't in the mood to deal with the psychology of that mental thought.

"What are you doing here, Jimmy?"

"Wanted to see if Caro would like to come to dinner with Tasha tonight." He gave a grin—a lewd one. "The little woman has cooked a big meal."

Declan wanted to refuse, it dangled along the tip of his tongue, but he didn't speak. He wasn't sure the words that would come out of his mouth would actually be comprehensible as opposed to a feral growl.

"Declan and I would love to go, thank you for the invitation. What time should we be there?" Caro's words yanked him from the mental image he had of snapping Jimmy in two pieces. Or was that into lots of little ones?

"What?" His question was mirrored by Jimmy.

"I'm sorry, I thought you were inviting us both. Wasn't that the case? This way Declan can drive us down and bring us back so you don't have to take more time away from your wife and kids." She stepped up beside Declan, her voice smooth and calm.

From the look on Jimmy's face, he'd planned on taking plenty of time away from them. With Caro.

Jimmy gave a smile and kept his attention riveted on Caro as opposed to meeting his gaze. "Well, I have space to take you down and back. I don't mind, I'm sure Declan has things to do."

Declan crossed his arms. "Actually, dinner would be a great break. I've been working hard all day. Tasha is one hell of a cook. Tell her we'll be there about six, unless you have changed the time you eat."

Caro moved to the door and slipped inside. The moment they were alone, Declan held Jimmy's stare. "I told you to leave her alone, Jimmy. No way in hell I let that woman ride anywhere with you, you nasty bastard. You should be fucking ashamed with the way you treat your marriage vows."

"You have some nerve preaching down to me, McBride. You were married."

He bristled as was his wont when someone mentioned his past marriage. "Was and I never cheated on her." *More than I can say for her but that's neither here nor there.*

Jimmy glared up at him before giving a soft snort and moving to his vehicle. He paused by the driver's door and Declan lifted his eyebrow in silent question.

"You can't protect her twenty-four hours a day, McBride. There will come a time when she's alone."

He bared his teeth. "If I find you have done a damn thing to her it will take them a long and arduous surgery to remove the tools I'll shove up your ass after I beat the shit out of you."

Jimmy paled but did his best not to show he had been rattled. "Are you threatening me?"

Declan shook his head and stepped closer so the only thing separating them was the truck. "I don't make threats, Jimmy. You'd be wise to not forget that piece of information."

His scowl deepened as he climbed in his truck then drove away. Declan didn't move from his spot until the tail lights had vanished from view. Content Jimmy had truly left, he pivoted and strode to the cabin's door and entered.

He heard her by the fireplace and walked to where he could actually place eyes on her. She knelt before the flames and stabbed at it with the poker, rearranging the newer pieces of wood she'd just added.

She peered at him over her shoulder, briefly, before returning her attention to the flickering fire before her. Her stiff posture told him she expected him to verbally attack her. He didn't wish to fight with her.

Not now. Instead of engaging with her, he went to his room with plans to shower to get the grime from the oil change off his body.

Walking from his room toward the bathroom, he spied her again. She stood there, staring through the glass. Her body language remained stiff yet he couldn't help but identify the softness that lingered beneath her hard posture. He knew how she felt against him. Writhing below him. Above him. Beside him.

Declan acted, didn't think about it, just went to her and swept her up in his arms before carrying her to the tub with him where he stripped her and put her beneath the hot shower.

Chapter Seven

Caro tapped out a fast cadence with her left foot standing by the living room window. True, she normally didn't mind the silence for she worked in it daily. But this… This was not work.

"No work. No friends. Just him."

Him. Declan McBride. The cop.

Even just thinking about him had her pussy readying for sex. The slickness grew between her thighs as her nipples drew painfully tight. She increased the cadence before throwing her hands up and stomping to the kitchen where she stared at the coffee pot.

Declan had left her here while he went to town. She blew out a frustrated breath and filled the kettle then placed it on the burner.

"Man's been in a mood since we got back from supper with Tasha. His mood went downhill every time Jimmy looked at me." She swiped a mug and set it on the counter.

"Not like I asked that bastard to leer at me or anything." She rummaged for a tea bag and added it along with three spoonfuls of sugar and a slice of lemon.

"Didn't show it to anyone but me either. Man's good."

And he was. Professional all the way around. But the glares he had given her—alone—reminded her nothing of the man who could—and did—deliver her to heights of great passion. No trace of any kindness or even sympathy remained.

This morning, he'd not even argued. Just had said no to her question of accompanying him. Monotone. No. That was it. Nary a reason. He had just left.

"And now I'm alone again." She shut off the stove and grabbed the handle only to swear and jerk back. *Son of a... That hurt!*

Caro held her hand beneath a stream of icy water until the burn pain alleviated to where she could tolerate it. Nearly five minutes. She removed it from the water and—with a hot pad this time—filled her mug and let the tea steep as she went to the bathroom for a few things then returned to continue addressing the injury.

Caro sat at the table as she worked. Footsteps on the porch had her staring at the door. She scowled. *Damn man wants to go grocery shopping and take care of his things in that pissy little no account town without me then he can carry everything back in on his own.*

She paused in wrapping her hand with the gauze bandage and tilted her head. *I didn't hear his vehicle.* She'd already popped a few acetaminophen to reduce the pain and he could have driven up while she'd been in the bathroom rooting through his medicine cabinet.

Fear crept in. She slowly rose from her seat, tucking the edge of the gauze in, and began to exit the room when the knock came.

She wasn't sure what to do. Should she answer? Pretend she wasn't here? That the place was empty? Cripes, her heart pounded so hard. She grimaced over the nausea roiling within her gut.

Forcing herself to the door, she opened it. *Shit. Should have pretended I wasn't here.*

Jimmy stood there, flashing a perfect smile.

"Hello, Caro."

Two words. Two that made her wonder if she'd forgotten to actually put on any clothing today with the way it made her feel. And not naked in a good way. She was cold and wanted to shudder from his gaze. The sound of her name sliding from his lips made her skin crawl.

"Mr Harstone." She kept her injured hand behind the cabin door. "Something you needed?"

His grin turned leery and he raked her from head to toe with his gaze. "I waited for him to leave, you know."

This could get ugly fast. She ignored his comment. "Where's your truck?"

"Invite me in, Caro." His grin widened. "I saw how you watched me last night at dinner."

Watched him? Was he serious? "I think there's no reason for you to be here."

"Don't be like that. I saw the hunger. That prick isn't here now. You don't have to pretend you don't feel it as well and there's nothing between us."

He shifted and she watched him, scared to make a move.

"I promise I'll make you feel like no one ever will again."

Words she full heartedly believed. He already made her feel like no one else ever would. And she could honestly say, she wasn't a fan.

"Sorry. As exciting as the offer is, one you're a married man and that's just wrong. Two, this isn't my cabin and I don't feel right inviting you into his home. If you want to come in, you should return when he's back."

His smile was truly unpleasant. He stepped closer to her and she struggled not to move back. There wasn't anywhere she could go. She didn't have her boots on so running outside wasn't a smart option. Not to mention, Jimmy was between her and freedom. She couldn't call for Declan—he didn't have a phone in the house.

"I didn't come all this way to see him…" He tipped his head to the side. "I came to see you."

"Why me? I never gave you any indication I was interested in you. I'm actually fond of your wife. Why would you cheat on her?"

"She's a hick."

She's a lot better than you, bastard. "She's a sweet woman and the mother of your children."

"Tasha won't care." He stroked his chin. "I've wanted to taste that sweet dark skin ever since you strolled into the room that day we were here." He shifted his stance. "I know you're hell in the sack and can't wait to get you there again."

Irritation speared her and she went ramrod straight. "Excuse me?"

His grin flashed and she scowled at him. "No need to try and be coy. It's only us. I know all about you, Jasmine Hoyer. You have no need to keep up this pretense."

More fear surged up from the soles of her feet to cover her. "My name is Caro."

His expression turned evil. He stepped toward her and placed a hand on the door before shoving it open. "It's cold out here, let me in."

She stumbled back and winced when he slammed the door behind him. He sniffed and wiped his hand along his nose. "You know…" he said conversationally. "This could have been much easier on you."

"Why would you do this?"

"Because you seem to want to ignore how much sexual tension there is between us."

He moved closer and she retreated the same number of steps.

"It pissed me off seeing you standing there with him, acting as if you didn't know me, Jasmine. Acting as if you were somehow better than me when I'd been with you lying in that fleabag motel after we fucked and snorted our way through more money than I've seen in a long time."

This time it clicked in her head. Jasmine actually knew this bastard. *Never again will I pretend to be someone I'm not. This is just insane.*

He waved a hand at her as he shrugged out of his coat. "Just because you change your attire and adopt a new name doesn't mean I don't know you. Know how much you love your crank and coke. And let's not forget the rest of the shit I've known you to put in your body."

"What do you want?"

Lewd didn't even begin to describe the grin he gave. He leaned forward and rested his palms on the tabletop.

"You know what I want, Jasmine. You know how I like it. Rough. Don't worry, I won't leave any marks on you for your bodyguard to see. But I will have you on your knees before me, shoving my cock down your throat. Watching your eyes bulge out as you struggle to breathe. You know how much that turns me on. You as well. I know how you like that asphyxiation play."

Could her dread get worse? Probably. And knowing her luck, it would.

"This isn't happening. Not here. You want to have dirty nasty sex you come back to Atlanta. Find me there."

"Why should I? You're here. I'm here. You can't tell me he doesn't know you're a whore. He sleeping with you as well?"

She didn't know how to respond. Jimmy glared at her. "You slut. You are spreading your legs for him. I thought you didn't like him."

He moved closer and she picked up the scissors, pretending to have done it without thought.

"Or are you hoping for a little leeway back in the city if you give it up to him now?"

She gave a small shrug and he laughed.

"You have to leave, Jimmy. I can't let him find you here."

He puffed out his chest. "I'm not scared of him. He has no jurisdiction here."

Somehow she didn't think that would stop Declan from beating him into a bloody pulp.

"When will you get a chance to make it back to Atlanta?" *I'm never visiting there again.*

"Not for a while. Hard to get away from her."

"You seem to do fine out here."

He sat across from her and she breathed a bit easier.

"Are you jealous?"

Dear sweet Jesus. Hell no. Another little smile was all she allowed. *Declan, please don't be long.*

* * * *

"My other witness is dead."

Cold settled around Declan's heart at those words from Jackie. "How'd it happen?"

"I don't know." Jacqueline sounded beyond pissed. "He was at a safe house as well but that blew up this morning."

Declan knew she'd be pacing her office. Each step sharp and calculating. "The officer guarding him?"

"Dead. They're all dead. Jasmine is my last witness and I need her here. Yesterday."

"Get a forty-eight hour extension."

"Forty-eight? Are you kidding me?"

"Do it, Jackie. We'll be there and meet you in front of the courthouse but you have to buy us the time."

"Damn you, McBride. One, stop calling me Jackie, and two, why the hell weren't you ever this passionate about your career when we were married?"

"I was. My passion just didn't need to come with a detective's badge. I'll be there in two days with her."

"So help me if you leave me hanging out to dry." Her tone once again was ice cold.

"I know all about how you are, Jackie. No need for threats." He hung up and swore. They'd lost another brother.

"What's wrong?" Martin asked from behind him.

"Time for us to leave."

"So soon?"

He faced his old friend. "Yes, I'm afraid so. She has an appointment she can't miss."

"Does she know Jimmy?"

Declan struggled to hide his distaste at that name. "Why do you ask?"

"He's been to Atlanta a few times. Wasn't sure if they knew one another."

He shrugged. "It's a big city, Martin. Neighbors don't always know one another."

"Sure thing. Just figured it was a possibility."

Declan would be lying if he didn't think it was one now. *No way, that's just too much of a coincidence.* Problem was, he didn't believe in them. Most of the people who lived here had done so most of their lives or had moved from neighboring towns. Not having come from Atlanta.

"I have to get going, Martin. Thanks for everything."

"You do what you have to. I'll take care of your cabin."

The men shook hands and Declan gave him a smile. "Thanks, man."

"I know it's none of my business, son, but I like her for you. Aside from this phone call you seem happy around her. She's good for you."

"I'm just protecting her, Martin."

"Sure thing, son. Sure thing. You keep telling yourself that." They walked to the door.

She's a drug addict and thief. "Bye, old man."

"See you around, youngster."

He waved over his shoulder as he jogged down the shoveled steps to his waiting Jeep. Declan didn't waste time getting back to the cabin. He'd brought her here to keep her safe but having heard what he had, it had rattled him a bit. He needed to see she was okay for himself.

The two bags of groceries in his hand, he strode from the Jeep to the door and pushed it open. Both bags slipped to the floor and spilled free. Seconds later he had his service weapon palmed and he searched through the cabin for her. A search that didn't take long yet ended in a way he didn't wish for it to. No sign of Jasmine.

He grabbed his thicker jacket and stared past the overturned table. His rifle was gone from where it usually rested. On the floor were medical supplies, intermixed with broken shards of ceramic mug.

Shit! He checked his ammunition and went to the porch. Two sets of prints led away from the cabin heading toward the woods. One he recognized as male and the other—more drag marks than anything. He bit off another oath and set out at a trot, weapon in hand.

The first drop of brilliant red blood upon the pristine white snow was a knife to his heart. Farther on more dotted the crust that he continued to burst through with his progression. Declan picked up his speed.

A cry pierced the air and he frowned as he broke into a run. It wasn't a woman's cry. He neared and burst into the open, weapon ready to fire.

"Caro?"

The woman in question stood over a prone body, a large thick branch in one hand. Caro faced him, yet he was sure she didn't see him. Her left hand had been bandaged.

"You ever cut me again, you dick sucker, and I'll feed you that little swizzle stick in pieces."

Blatant. "Caro?" he tried again as he approached. Blood dripped down over her hand that held the branch.

She looked up at him, hesitated for a few seconds before running to him and launching herself into his arms. Her body trembled and he didn't want to release her. However, he did. He had to deal with this person before he could focus his attention on her.

"Stay behind me." His order was brisk and unemotional.

Before he had even gotten to the man, he knew the identity of the one who lay there. Jimmy. He approached, weapon trained.

"Jimmy." He ensured there was no danger to him. Jimmy's hands were out to his sides, so if there was a weapon the man lay upon it. "Jimmy." Still nothing.

Was he dead? Declan crouched beside him and checked for a pulse. It was there.

"Jimmy."

The man stirred and groaned. Blood dribbled from the back of his head. Caro had cracked him a good one.

"You filthy whoring bit—"

Jimmy's eyes widened as he stared up the barrel of Declan's pistol.

Declan shoved his Glock into the back of his waistband. "I warned you." His voice trembled with the need for violence.

From the panic in Jimmy's gaze, Declan saw that he realized and understood said threat. "It's not like I haven't fucked her before."

Rage. There was no other word to describe the unending pulse that moved through him.

Declan punched him in the jaw taking minute pleasure in noting how his head snapped to the side. He longed to do more. To feel the bones in Jimmy's body shatter and break as he pummeled him. To be witness to the blood streaming from his body.

He did nothing of the sort for he still had a job to do. Declan stole a glance at Caro. Jasmine. Her eyes sparked with anger and fear.

"Let's go." He stood and hefted the unconscious Jimmy over his shoulder. "Leave the branch."

"I'll keep it, thanks."

Declan was furious. At everything. How he'd missed her connection to Jimmy. The fact that another officer had died because of this case. That Jimmy had slept with Jasmine—a woman he was personally becoming way too serious about. The fact that she had never divulged to him her past with the man he now carried through the snow.

No words were exchanged until they reached the cabin. He secured Jimmy and laid him on the couch.

Had they had sex on his couch today while he'd been in town? New anger poured in.

"Pack."

She didn't speak and he turned only to pause. She looked like hell, standing in the kitchen among the broken mug and sticky residue from her drink. Her hands shook, and he walked toward her.

"Are you okay?" Damn it, his voice was gruff.

"Do I fucking look okay to you?"

This was the Jasmine he remembered…and couldn't stand.

"You look like hell." The devil in him stirred to life blowing on the simmering embers of the green-eyed monster within. "What made you decide to hit him? Lovers' spat?"

Crack!

She caught him unawares and he felt the bite of her slap.

"Bastard." She was radiant in her fury.

He stared at her bandaged hand then up to the now exposed cut on her arm. He narrowed his gaze. "What happened?"

"This is your fault," she snapped. "Because you didn't want me in town with you. You left me alone and defenseless. He showed up here, without a vehicle, and forced his way in here. When I wouldn't strip down for him and fuck him he flipped his shit. Don't you dare ask me if we had a lovers' spat." Her voice shook and this time he knew it was from fear, not anger.

"What happened to your hand and how did you get cut?" Declan had to focus on her or he'd go back and put another fist in Jimmy's face.

"I burned my hand. Was bandaging it up when that fuck showed up."

"But you knew him."

"What? You wanted me to say something about it before his wife when we had dinner together? Would that have been better for you?"

Grudgingly he saw her point. "Could still have mentioned it after the fact. We have to get going. They need you at the courthouse." He frowned when the clock on his coffee maker went dark. The hum from the refrigerator also fell silent. "We need to go now."

He grabbed her uninjured arm and pulled her to the back. "Pack some things quick." He shoved her in that direction and as she went, he used his foot to nudge the man on his couch. Jimmy stirred and looked up at him, furious.

"Where's my rifle?" Declan attuned to every noise and waited for her to return.

"Fuck you," Jimmy spat at him.

"You know you're a pig. But cutting her and kidnapping her, you'll pay for that."

"She was mine long before she was ever yours, Declan. Remember that every time you want to put your dick into her. Mine was there first. I was even

107

with her when she got the heart tattoo on her ass. I used to pull out of her and cover it with my cum. Just like her back and sometimes her face. Marking my territory. You can call her Caro all you want but she was mine first. And you'll never be able to forget that. We even fucked on your bed. She screamed my name to the roof as I pounded her."

"Who did you call?"

Caro walked into the room, a small bag in hand.

"Jimmy! Who did you call?"

"Just someone who contacted me and asked if I'd seen her."

"When did you call?" The man shook his head. "When?"

"Yesterday. They said they weren't going to hurt her, just wanted to ask her a question or two."

"They don't want to hurt her, they want to kill her." Declan punched him then cut his ties before beckoning to Caro. "Let's go. We have to get out of here."

"What about him?"

He ignored his jealousy. "I'll let Martin know he's here. Or he can leave when he comes to." He grabbed what he needed—it took him barely a minute—and they were running across the snow to the shed when the first shots rang out.

Declan rammed through the door with his Jeep as they took off down his drive. "Keep your head down!"

She didn't argue, just crouched low and did her best not to get in his way as they slipped and slid over the snowy ground.

He drifted onto the road before shifting and gunning the engine. Steering with one hand, he used his other to grab his phone. After placing a swift call to Martin he dropped the phone on the seat by her and concentrated on getting them away alive. Bullets thudded into his vehicle side and windows as they raced away.

Declan knew he had to get to the plane but figured that route was blocked right now, so he had to get somewhere else first then go there. Whipping off onto an old logging road, he got them up to the small shack that was there. Not much to look at but it would give him what he needed for the moment. Time.

He hid the Jeep as best he could and led a still silent woman inside. The place had no heat and he watched her shiver.

"You okay?" He stared at her.

"Not hit if that's what you're asking."

He hated the quiver in her voice and wanted to take it away. Still, he couldn't let Jimmy's words go from his head. "Did you fuck him in my house?"

Chapter Eight

Caro blinked a few times and stared at the man standing before her looking like he wanted to spit nails. Surely he wasn't seriously asking her that. Not when she'd just been dragged from his cabin, cut, shot at and was currently standing in a cold ass rickety building she wasn't sure would hold up against the next strong wind. Her mouth moved but no words came out.

"Answer me." Declan's tone brooked no room for argument.

She was grateful she'd taken the time to slap some bandages on her arm before leaving the cabin for he sure didn't appear to be concerned about her.

"Really? That's what you want to know? Not about how the hell we get those shooting at us off our ass? You want to know if I fucked him in your house."

"In my bed?"

She wanted to snap back at him, truly she did, but she kept it contained behind her teeth—seriously clenched teeth. When Jimmy had first shown up she'd thought he had been lying through his teeth. She had discovered he hadn't been—apparently her twin truly had screwed this man.

I could end this right now by telling him the truth. There was no reason to do so. They were on their way back now so—God willing—once they made it there safely, she'd trade places back with her twin and could get on with her own life.

"Well?"

"No," she answered truthfully. "I did no such thing."

"He said you did."

"If you were going to believe him anyway then why ask me in the first place? Just get me back to Atlanta so I don't have to look at you again." She rubbed her arms and wished for a sweatshirt beneath her coat.

"They'll be coming after us here. We'll wait until they do then take their vehicle—we have a better chance of making it to the airstrip if they think we're one of them."

Them. *Who the fuck is them?* She couldn't push that question free—supposedly she knew who was after her.

"Fine." She gazed around and found a chair, which she sat in.

"Why didn't you tell me about you and Jimmy?" He paced back and forth, occasionally checking the window.

Because I didn't know. "We all have secrets. Why didn't you tell me you'd been married before?"

He froze and whirled toward her. "Who told you that?"

"Doesn't matter. You didn't tell me."

"My life isn't up for debate. My past is my past."

She crossed her arms and held his intimidating stare. "So is mine."

"You slept with Jimmy."

She hid her shudder. *As if that would ever happen.* "I also did drugs according to the file you have on me, so why don't we chalk it up to my making stupid asinine decisions and let it go."

"You didn't touch him?"

"I can't say that."

His gaze narrowed and for a moment she allowed herself to believe he was jealous.

"Why not?"

"You saw me standing over him with a branch. I touched him all right. Hit the bastard, that's touching." She held up a hand to ward off what she knew was coming next. "No I didn't sleep with him while you were gone. I didn't want to let him in your cabin but he shoved his way in." She swallowed. "For a while I kept him on the other side of the table talking then he got bored with that and…" Nope, she didn't want to go through it again. He had seen the mess in his place. "I already told you this."

"Are you okay?" Declan's tone was softer this time and she wanted to have him hold her but refrained from any kind of movement.

"Fine."

"Good. Get under that table and don't come out until I tell you it's okay to do so."

He chambered a round in his pistol, and she followed his order immediately. Faintly, she could make out the sound of an engine. Squeezing her eyes shut, she prayed for this to be over.

I'm never leaving Wisconsin again. Stuff doesn't happen to me there. I'll work and I'll go home. That's it. Nothing more.

Doors slammed and she jerked once the shooting started. Bullets thudded into the floor around her.

Glass shattered above and wood splintered as the walls barely slowed the projectiles as they cut through. Making herself as small as possible, she bit her lower lip and did her best not to scream aloud in fear.

The sounds of fists hitting flesh reached her. It seemed it fell silent as swiftly as it had begun. She remained crouched beneath the metal desk, ducked as far into the corner of it as she could. Behind the side of drawers. Solitary footsteps neared and she burrowed her head against her knees, continuing to keep her eyes scrunched.

"Come on out, Caro."

Declan's voice sent a rush of relief through her. Unfortunately, her limbs wouldn't move. She'd wedged herself in there so tight and had sat so tense, now they weren't cooperating.

"Caro?"

"I can't move."

A few seconds then his face filled the opening as he stared in at her. Those amazing eyes of his held concern. He offered her his hand and she shakily took it, allowing him to tug her free. Once out, her legs still didn't want to cooperate and she reached for the desktop to keep from falling only she didn't quite reach it.

Declan, however, *was* there. He smelled faintly of gunpowder, sweat and man. She didn't even pretend she didn't need his strength right then. Just held onto him and buried her face in his chest. He wrapped both arms around her and held on.

"You'll be fine, Caro, but we have to move."

She may have imagined the brush of his firm lips along her ear but she had no intentions of letting that go. He didn't let her pull completely away from him.

"No need to stare at this all," he whispered as he led her through the room and out into the cold.

She didn't argue and trusted him to guide her to where they had to go. The strong beat of his heart soothed her. When he opened a door and helped her up into the passenger seat, she opened her eyes and looked around. *Christ, it looks like a movie.* All the bodies lying on the ground, their blood mixing with the snow, churned her stomach. She averted her gaze and stared out over the hood of the blue and white older SUV.

It roared to life and she groaned with relief as heat pumped through the vents. Holding her hands over the nearest one, she sniffed as Declan shifted the vehicle into gear and backed up, turned around and got them back on the road.

Darkness covered them swiftly and she tried not to cry. This day had just been a bit much for her. No, she didn't need coddling but she wouldn't say no to a nice warm shower and bed. Perhaps some nice comfort food as well.

"Fuck!"

Declan's single word had her tensing all over again. What was going on? She hadn't a clue.

"This guy really wants you dead."

Great. She kept her mouth firmly shut, well aware if it opened, she'd puke all over the interior.

She saw the headlights in the side mirror. They closed in with incredible speed and she whimpered when the vehicles collided. Again and again the one behind hit into them and she couldn't help the scream this time when they rolled off the road and toward the edge of the mountain. They teetered on the side for a brief heart-stopping moment before sliding on.

* * * *

Declan stirred and winced at the pain that lanced up his side. He touched his head and drew his fingers away, tacky with his blood. What the hell had happened? He took a moment and tried to sort through the events that had put him in this predicament.

Protection. Running. Shooting. Caro.

He couldn't see anything because of the inky darkness surrounding them. Not even the headlights were on. "Caro?" He reached out one arm and sought her in the dark. Nothing.

"Caro? Sweetheart, I need you to answer me if you can hear me. I can't see you. Are you okay?" He struggled to unhook his seatbelt, grunting at the impact of him hitting the roof when he was finally freed. They were upside down and he moved cautiously against the roof to where she should be. One of her hands hit him in the face. Moving with instinct, he unhooked her belt and caught her weight as she collapsed onto him.

He lay there, arms around her as he checked for a pulse in her neck. She had one and he breathed in relief. The wind rocked them and he stiffened when the vehicle slid forward slightly.

Shit. I have to get us out of here. Problem was, he didn't know where they were, or what was outside. That didn't matter. All he truly knew was they couldn't stay in here and slip to whatever was below. He inched back and tried the handle on the door. It creaked open and he squinted against the swirling snow. Keeping the still unresponsive Caro against his chest, he continued on until they were fully free of the overturned SUV.

It may have been longer but to him it didn't much feel like it when the vehicle tipped and slipped down. He shivered and wrapped his arms tighter around the still unmoving woman in his embrace. As he continued moving them back, inch by cautious inch, he ran over what possessions they had.

Their clothes. At least each still had on their coat. No hats, though. He had his Glock, he could feel the handgrip pressing into the small of his back as he inched along. The wind whipped the snowflakes around and they stung like little bees as they struck his exposed skin. With one hand he turned up the collar of his coat and curved his fingers inside the sleeve. He had no gloves.

"Mmm."

He froze at the low groan from Caro. Two more escaped her before she stirred.

"What happened?" Caro asked in a rasped tone, like she'd taken a punch to the throat.

Or the snap of a seatbelt across her throat. "We went over the road. SUV's gone over and we need to get up to the road and find a way to the airport so we can get back to Atlanta. How are you feeling?"

"Like I went over the edge in a car accident." She shifted. "Why am I lying on you?"

"You were unresponsive and I had to get you out of the vehicle."

"I can't see shit."

"Me either. And no, I don't know where we are."

"Damn. What about the ones who were after us?"

"Haven't heard a peep from them, if they're still up there. They may very well have continued on their way once we went over." She got off him but didn't go far—her leg against his told him that.

"So what do we do?"

116

"Are you okay?"

"Head hurts but I don't think there're any broken bones, if that's what you are asking." A moment of silence. "What about you?"

"Same."

"Okay, so we can move. But to where and how? I can't see a damn thing and I don't know where the edge is."

"I'm going back from where the truck went over. Slowly." He fixed his other sleeve to protect his hands. "Keep as much of your body covered as you can."

"Do you want your gloves?"

He'd been moving again but stopped. "My gloves?"

"Yeah, I took a pair of yours from the cabin before we left."

Hell yes he wanted them. His fingers were crying in agony. "You need to keep them."

"Do—" She grabbed his arm and worked her way down. "You don't even have any protection. Take them."

"No."

"Look, it's smarter that way. My clothes are bigger, I can wrap them in my sweatshirt. You have a gun, I'd just rather your fingers not be frozen when the time comes for you to be needing to pull a trigger."

"We'll share." He nearly groaned as the warmth surrounded his digits. "Fingers okay?" he asked.

"All wrapped up in my shirt and long-sleeved shirt. Then the coat sleeve. I'm fine. Let's get the hell out of here."

A few tics of time later and she wrapped a scarf around his neck.

"What are you doing?"

"I have a hood in this coat. I'm guessing you have nothing since you left in your bomber jacket." Her lips brushed his skin. "Don't worry, it's not hot pink."

He wouldn't have cared. It stopped more of the buffeting snow and wind. "Thank you."

They worked together in mostly silence until he could feel the hard packed road beneath his feet. Helping her up to stand beside him, Declan wrapped an arm around her. She leaned against him without a word.

"What now?"

"I could use a break from this weather. Let's see if can't find some shelter then figure out where we are and how to get to the airport from here."

"Sounds like a plan." She hooked her arm through his and yawned.

Declan thought about where they'd been when the car had first begun nudging them. There should be an abandoned cabin not too far from where they were. He struck out and she came with. Her body trembled beside his but she never once made a complaining peep.

It had been a while since he'd been there but he still managed to find the cabin within the hour. Or what remained of it. Not even a full four walls but there was a bit of barricade from the winds and cold as they sank down and huddled close.

"Tired," she muttered.

"Stay awake, Caro. I can't have you falling asleep on me here."

"Just a short nap? I'll let you take one after."

"No. We can't risk falling asleep."

"Right. Hypothermia." She moved closer. "So what? Wanna strip naked and share body heat?"

"I would love to," he said candidly. "Not going to happen, though. We just need to rest our legs a bit before we press on." He touched his head wound, grateful to discover it had stopped bleeding.

"So we're supposed to sit here and not fall asleep?"

Her tone made him chuckle. "Exactly."

"Okay, so talk to me then."

He fought his own yawn. "About what?"

"Christ, man, I don't care. Anything to keep me from falling asleep."

"Tell me about you and Jimmy."

She stiffened. "Okay, let's not talk about anything. He's off the table. If I'm about to die, I don't want to do it with that prick on my mind."

He smiled slightly. "So what then?"

"Tell me about you being married before."

Not a topic he wanted to go through but, hell, why not? "Very well. I wasn't married but a few years."

"Who. To whom?"

"The ADA prosecuting the case you're part of."

He didn't hear a peep out of her for two and a half minutes. "You were married to the woman prosecuting. The ADA."

He nodded. "Yep. Jacquelyn Ashcraft."

"So what happened?"

Any other situation and he would have shut her down, not wanting to expound on the dissolution of his marriage. But it was what it was.

"We'd married when I was new to the force. Later on, it was apparent she wasn't content being with just an officer."

"Aren't you still an officer?"

"I am. She wanted me to become a detective and move up the ladder. I was then, and still am now, content with walking a beat. I like where I am." He flexed his toes. "So she moved on as she continued to move up. It wouldn't do for a woman angling to become the next District Attorney to have a regular cop as a husband. So she left me and our small place and moved uptown."

"Bitch."

Her heartfelt sentiment had him smiling, full-fledged this time. "She's always been after something more. I was a mere mortal in her way of becoming immortal."

"So she ditched you and wanted her gilded cage."

"Pretty much. This case will most likely cement her bid for DA if it goes well."

"I see." Her words were subdued.

"You are way different than I thought you'd be in a situation like this."

Her bark of self-deprecating laughter was anything but amusing. "Yeah, it's like I'm a whole other person."

"It is. And since we're putting all cards out, I like this persona better, much better, than the Jasmine I first met."

She muttered something that sounded a lot like 'me too' before giving a noncommittal grunt.

With a bit more energy, he helped her up and took five seconds kissing her before saying, "Let's get this over with."

Chapter Nine

Bones had been replaced by icicles. Caro wasn't sure she'd ever be warm again. She drew her arms inside her clothes and shoved her freezing fingers beneath her armpits. They'd walked and rested then walked some more.

I'd put my toes under here too. Her feet cried for warmth. "How much farther?"

"Few miles."

"This is like walking along Mendota in eighty below."

"What?"

Shit. I have to be careful what I say. The cold is addling my brain. "Just muttering." She definitely had to be more careful. It wouldn't do to be talking about a lake in Madison, Wisconsin, when she was supposed to be from Atlanta.

If he had any suspicions he didn't share them. "Need a break?"

"Yes. And a car. Some thick socks fresh from the dryer." She grinned at the thought. "After a hot shower. Oh, God, a nice steamy hot bath."

"Didn't you just say shower?"

Semantics. "Changed my mind. I want to be submerged in the water. Have it surround me in a cocoon of warmth."

"Wine as well?"

"No. Hot toddie."

He drew her close. How he managed to exude such heat in their current situation, she had no clue. "And are you alone?"

Her body responded. Apparently it wasn't so cold. "I may have room…for a cop. Might be a tight fit, though, so we'd be in close proximity."

"How close?" His warm breath teased her ear.

"Very. Fitting close like a puzzle piece."

"Sounds like heaven to me."

"Yes it does."

He kissed her and she sagged into him. His strong arms banded around her, anchoring her to his unending strength.

"Then let's get there."

She longed to cry by the time she saw the outlying lights for the small airstrip.

"Damn it."

Two words she had no wish to hear. She crouched beside him, bracing her arm against him. "Those trucks shouldn't be there, should they?"

"Nope."

"Don't they think we're dead? Why are they waiting there?" She desperately wanted them to go away and leave her the fuck alone. Go so she could begin to thaw out and remember what it was like to have feeling in her limbs.

"Reckon because they are scared of their boss and don't want to risk anything going wrong."

"But how would he know if they waited or not?"

"When you show up in court that man will know you weren't stopped here. They killed the other witness. Jackie told me that when I talked to her before we left."

"You talked to her before we left?"

"Yes."

Why did that knowledge fill her with jealousy? *I'll chalk it up to the cold because there's no way in hell I'm thinking straight.*

"So what do we do now?"

"I say we head for one of the smaller outbuildings and get out of the wind for a bit then decide how we're going to overtake them and steal a plane."

"Can you fly?"

"Yes."

Her brow rose at that. Another piece to the man puzzle of one Declan McBride. Cop. Amazing lover. Pilot.

They moved slowly down and she was actually thankful to the wind as it howled around them for it masked the sound of the door squeaking open. They slipped through into the dark building. She could see a bit more since one of the tall outside lights was near but there wasn't complete ease of seeing around them. She saw several desk shapes, a few chairs and outlines of shelving units.

Caro didn't move until Declan had checked the entire thing. The cold still lingered but, considering that she no longer trudged through deep snow and fought off brutal wind, she was fine.

"We're good. Stay away from the window, though."

"Sure."

She avoided the chair and sat on the desk, feet off the cold floor. Moments later, Declan sat next to her and wrapped an arm around her.

"What's the plan?"

"I need to get a phone and discover how many are out there."

"There should be a phone in here. I mean, it's an office."

"You're right. Let's look, just be careful."

"My new middle name." She slid off and went to the side away from the window. There was another small room and she stepped inside and shut the door behind her. Then she flipped on the light. A bathroom.

Swiftly she took care of emptying her bladder then took out some paper towels and stared at the dried blood on her head as she washed her hands. Turning on the water, she waited for it to get hot. Declan knocked.

"You okay?"

She shut off the light and opened the door, drew him in and shut it behind him. Then she hit the switch again. The man took up a good bit of the room in there. He wore her red scarf and she saw blood on him as well.

"You need to wipe off that blood." She wetted the towels in her hand and beckoned him closer. Declan stepped around her and sat on the closed toilet lid. She did her best to be gentle as she got off the dried blood.

The hot water began to steam up the room but she didn't shut it off. The warmth felt wonderful. The small room allowed their own body heat to add to it as well.

Declan stood up and took the wet wad from her hand then tossed it in the trash. He drew her close and unzipped her coat. She returned the favor and sought out his skin beneath his shirt.

Everything but the two of them faded. This was about nothing more than the two of them being grateful they were alive. His lips proved to be too much of a temptation for her and she pulled him to her mouth. Needing to feel him.

In a heartbeat it went from gentle to dominating. Caro didn't mind. This man, this cop allowed her what she needed. He lifted her and pressed her against the wall. She wrapped her legs around his waist and moved her arms to hook around his neck.

"Caro," he rasped.

She shifted against him. "Please."

They exploded, tearing at clothing until she moaned with pleasure as the thick head of his cock nudged into her. Caro's eyelids fluttered and she exhaled as he filled her.

Declan rested one hand against the wall at her head. His other he had between them as he played with her clit. Light flicks had Caro grinding against his shaft.

"Move," she panted.

He did with a swift pinch to her clit. Caro dug her hands into his broad shoulders and bit her lower lip as he stroked deep and hard. Their grunts filled the air as they both catapulted down toward the end they craved.

Long powerful thrusts. Behind them the steam continued to build in time with the passion. She closed her eyes and rode it out. Words weren't needed. This was not tender. Not slow and gentle. This contained a desperate edge. Almost like they both knew it would be the last time.

He released her clit and put her hand there instead. When his fingers sank into her hips she mewled and played with herself.

"So fucking sexy." His words were low and drawn out.

Caro opened her eyes and found him watching where they were joined. His gaze blazed when he met hers and she flexed her internal muscles. His grin was feral and she gasped when he increased his speed. His jaw was set, his muscles in his neck drawn taut as he fucked her.

The release raced over her, spreading throughout her entire body, and she bowed, a keening cry escaping before he slammed his mouth upon hers, silencing her. One, two, three more strokes before his seed filled her.

He remained buried inside her as they both fought for breath. Against her, his heart pounded as hard as her own. The kiss gentled and he eventually drew back.

"What?" His unrelenting gaze sort of unnerved her.

"I want you again." He thrust his hips. "And again. I can't get enough of you, Jasmine."

Had he stripped her naked and plunged her outside in the wind and snow, she couldn't have been any colder than she was right then. Forcing her expression to remain neutral, she gave a shrug. "Don't we have a plane to catch?"

He withdrew and placed her on the floor. They cleaned up swiftly and she shut off the hot water after dressing. She wanted to cry but she refused to allow any tears to fall.

You brought this on yourself, Caro. You made the decision to go along with this charade and the man has no reason not to buy you being your twin.

He held her stare and dragged a knuckle down her cheek before hitting the switch and plunging them into darkness before he opened the door. They went to separate ends and began looking for the phone.

She located it and lifted the receiver checking for a dial tone. "Declan."

"Find one?"

"Yes."

He was beside her in no time and she handed him the phone. She listened as he dialed a number and asked for Lieutenant Meltzer.

"No I'm not in the air yet," Declan said. "We were shot at, run off the road and now I have three vehicles out there that I'd bet anything aren't a welcoming party that we'd want to run into."

She poked at her hand still wrapped in gauze. The burn didn't feel any better and she rolled her eyes as she stopped.

"No, dammit. We need a plane. We'll never get out of here. Best I can do is disable two of the three vehicles and steal the third then try for the next airstrip. Get a plane there ready and fueled up for us. We'll be coming in hot, I'm sure."

He hung up and spoke several extremely colorful words. Caro didn't move.

"I need you to stay here while I go out there."

"Okay."

"Not going to argue with me?"

"Hell no. I will be right here."

"I'll be right back."

His shadow moved away and through the door. The moment he had closed it behind him, she picked up the phone and dialed her cell.

"Hello?"

"You had better be there, Jasmine," she hissed into the receiver. "Courthouse tomorrow."

"Caro?"

"Who else would it be? I can't believe what you've gotten me into. Make sure you're there. Don't make me come looking for you."

"Are you okay?"

"No. I'm not. Be there early, I'm not sure what time we're arriving. Stay hidden but make sure you come out when we arrive. And bring me my bag."

Silence met her demand and Caro glared at the mental visual of her twin.

"I'll be there, Caro."

She hung up with a muttered, "You'd better be." Caro wrapped her arms around her legs and rested her head on her knees. "Then I can get out of this mess and go home."

The door squawked announcing his return. "Let's go."

Back to those two words. She pushed to her feet, shoved any and all emotion for the man to the rear burner and joined him out in the cold. He took her hand and ran for the nearest vehicle. Opening one door, he practically shoved her through to the passenger side, started the motor then got them going. She could see men pouring from the main building, guns blazing and she just ducked. No point in screaming, it would likely only bother Declan and she just needed him to get them elsewhere safely.

"Tell me something about you I don't know."

His sentence shocked her and she looked over at him, strong features highlighted by the dash lights.

"Something you don't know about me? I thought the file had everything in it." Yes, she sounded bitter.

"Tell me."

"I have degrees in synthetic and structural chemistry and in macromolecular and polymer chemistry."

She ignored the gaze boring into her. "Nothing about that in the file."

Caro shrugged. "Not my fault. You told me to tell you something you didn't know. I told you."

"I'm not talking about the meth you make, that doesn't make you a PhD."

Her eye twitched. "Me either." *Guess my twin and I do have something in common. Chemistry.*

Couldn't the woman tell him the truth? Sure, cooking up drugs did give you a bit of a chemist edge but what she claimed... Not hardly. There was absolutely no record of Jasmine Hoyer having gone to even a community college. They'd checked her out.

Why do I have feelings for this woman? Why can't it just go back to the animosity we shared in the past?

He knew the answer. Because he'd crossed a line while out there in his cabin. One he never should have but had. And because of that, he'd allowed himself for a moment to believe she was different from what was down on paper. There was one person he could blame and if he looked in the rear-view, he would see that person looking back at him. So he didn't look.

"Right." The day he believed she had a PhD would be a cold day in hell. *Well, it is cold out and you've gone through hell to get to where you are.* He ignored his brains commentary.

"You asked."

Damn if she didn't sound hurt by his skepticism. "So I did."

Declan constantly checked the area around them, expecting another attack. It definitely hadn't been fortuitous for him to take her directly to a place where one of her ex-lovers resided. Why had Jimmy ratted them out? *Really? Jimmy's a druggie and a bastard. He'd sell anything for money or his next score.*

His brain had the right of it. He slanted his gaze askew to the woman riding with him. Shit, even now she prompted a visceral reaction from him. *I can control my lust.*

Declan wasn't positive about that but he would try his best. He refocused on the information he had. Could she be in on this? Immediately he dismissed the idea. She hadn't had any opportunity to get calls out. He'd made sure. Hell, his cabin had had the phone removed before they'd even arrived. So no way she'd gotten anything out to someone else.

Maybe something had passed between her and Jimmy that he had gotten something done or sent off for her? And then he had stopped back by to collect payment?

He wanted to groan in frustration. *What did all this leave me with?*

One huge fucking mess is what it leaves me with. Declan grunted and slowed down as they went around another curve.

"Do you remember ever seeing Jimmy with any of Kazakova's men?"

"No."

"Think. I'm trying to figure out who told them where we were."

"I can't help you."

He frowned. "More like won't."

"If I knew I would tell you."

He had his doubts. "So all you and Jimmy did was drugs and fuck."

She didn't make any comeback and yet he knew she wanted to lash into him. He kept his next comment to himself. He watched her in his periphery. She sat stiff, unbending, and anger poured off her in waves. He let her stew.

"Should be in the air soon." He killed the lights as they entered the airport.

"Where's the plane?"

"Not sure, one of the hangars."

"So, how do we find it?"

Good question. He parked among the other vehicles but left the motor running. They were away from the light and he scanned the area trying to figure out how best to solve that puzzle.

"I don't know. I do know we're not going anywhere if we don't get out of here fast. This storm is getting much worse."

"So shouldn't we go before that happens?"

"I would think so." He turned toward her. "I have to check the hangars."

"Want me to create a diversion on the chance there are some waiting here for us? I can drive around and if they're watching they'll follow me. May buy you some more time to find the jet."

His gut clenched. "You have to be safe."

"If the safest place for me is out of here then, dammit, let me help so we can make it a reality."

He grabbed her forearm. "I don't think—"

"I can do this. All I have to do is drive slow around the buildings."

"And if they start shooting?"

"I hopefully can avoid them hitting me." She covered his hand with her own. "I can do this."

He didn't want to leave her. "I'll work in a counter-clockwise direction. If you see one of the doors opened that's the one."

"Okay, so I drive down the runway and what, you pick me up?"

"Something like that. Let's play it by ear. There may not be anyone here yet and when the plane is pulled out of the hangar you can just get on."

"Well let's go before there's too much snow for us to even take off. Do we have to file a flight plan?"

He slid toward her and drew her the rest of the way so they were almost on top of one another. Her features were mostly shadowed but he could see the left side of her face because of the dash lights. Cupping her cheek, he stroked along her skin with his thumb. Warm skin. Supple skin. Tempting skin.

Declan lowered his hand and cupped her waist then lifted her so that she straddled him. His cock placed between her legs and he struggled not to forget what they had to accomplish right now. She didn't speak, just threaded her fingers through his hair and tugged her scarf off his neck.

Their lips met and her moan whittled away at his control even further. Pulling back, he slid to his right more and lifted her off. Filing away all the memories of how it had been between them, he eliminated all connection between them.

"Ready for this?"

"Sure."

Her voice shook and he wished there was a way for him to make her feel more confident about this. It could go smoothly or it could be harrowing. And given they'd already been shot at as well as run off the road, he wasn't sure how much she had left in her.

"See you at the plane." One final glance and he slipped from the warmth into the cold night.

Jogging off, he glanced back in time to see her flick on the parking lights and begin moving. Not away from but toward where he was headed. He wanted to yell for her but realized what she was doing. Making it safer for him. If they thought she'd already gone that way they would be on the other side so he'd not be in danger.

Something they would discuss once in the air. *He* was supposed to be protecting *her*, not the other way around. Stowing his emotions, Declan got to work. The sooner he found a plane, the sooner they could get back to somewhere safe.

Chapter Ten

The darkness worried her. Each second she wondered if someone would jump out and cut her down with an automatic. *I honestly need to stop watching so many action movies. Perhaps I should just watch children's stuff now. Like Disney. Something which won't set my imagination into overtime and high gear when I feel scared.*

She snorted with laughter. Scared? Petrified would be a better and more apt word. Even though she had the heater on full and the interior was hot, she couldn't stop the trembles that rocked her body or the tremors in her hands as she drove slowly around the hangars.

Not sure why I'm feeling sorry for myself here that he didn't believe me when I told him what I did about Jimmy. Or rather what I didn't tell him. She didn't have any clue if that man could have ratted her out. Hell, she'd just met him, although apparently her sister had known him before and had done things with him she wouldn't ever consider.

"I don't need to be thinking about Jasmine and her poor decisions." She exhaled and focused again on the accumulating snow as she drove.

Coming around from the back of one of the hangars, she saw a door open and her heart pounded. He'd found a plane. She slowed and parked by one of the buildings, shutting off the lights. It was three buildings away.

"I could go around the back and park there." She nodded to herself and put the vehicle back in gear and did just that. This time when she parked, she killed the engine and leaped out, keys remaining in the ignition.

The cold immediately bit into her and she shoved her hands in her pockets as she inched her way up along the metal building. There were no overhead lights on when she made it to the door and she slipped in. A faint glow filtered down from the jet.

"Declan?"

"Get on the plane."

His voice came from somewhere, she couldn't pinpoint it. She didn't hesitate, just made her way up the few steps. She was alone one minute, he stood behind her the next and pulled the steps up before securing the door.

"Get a seat." He brushed by her and entered the cockpit. She followed and sat in the seat next to him, copying his motion of putting on a headset.

He barely glanced at her, just checked the numerous switches and panels around him. Caro sat on her hands, partially to keep their shaking a secret and because this stuff made no sense to her. She didn't want to mess something up by accidentally hitting it.

"Whose jet is this?" she asked, as he rolled them from the hangar.

"No clue." He flicked some switches and put his hands on the steering part.

Yoke. Wasn't that what they called it? She closed her eyes only to pop them open again. All she had seen was action movies in which explosions, gunfire and death took place at the airport and they were making her extremely nervous.

The snow blew at the windshield and she hoped to hell that he knew what he was doing. She cut her gaze to him, his expression exuding nothing but the utmost confidence. That relaxed her a bit and when they taxied down the runway, she wasn't as scared.

Declan got them smoothly up into the air and when he looked at her and smiled, then and only then did she allow herself to completely relax.

"It's going to be a long flight. Why don't you go get some sleep?"

She shook her head. "You can't sleep. Why would I?"

"Because you can."

"Nope. I'll stay awake with you. Do you want me to get you a drink or something like that?"

"Coffee would be great."

She unbuckled herself and slipped back into the main body of the plane. A low whistle left her as she took in the impressive jet. Private and plush.

"Someone's not going to be happy their plane was stolen." She walked past the dark wood and leather seats to a small kitchen area where she found the makings for coffee. As it brewed she made her way to the bathroom where she stared at her reflection. Black circles beneath her eyes. She appeared exhausted. *What do you know, I am exhausted.*

"At least the blood is gone."

She washed her hands and dried them before heading back out. The temperature was comfortable enough and she removed her coat. Caro fixed his coffee and carried it back to the cockpit where she slipped in only to pause as he spoke to someone on the radio.

He gave her a brief smile but didn't stop talking. She sat and put his drink within reach.

"Thank you," he said softly.

She buckled herself back in and stared at the instrument panel. Well lit and far too complicated for her tired brain to make sense of. She closed her eyes as his warm soothing voice flowed over her.

"There are beds back there. Or seats that may be more comfortable."

She turned her head and opened her eyes. "You want me to leave?"

"No, I just wanted you to know you don't have to sleep up here."

"I'm not sleeping."

"Eyes closed and deep breathing. What would you call it?"

"If you must know I'm thinking about synthetic polymers. I call it relaxing."

His jaw flexed along with his fingers. She didn't blink as he reached for and drank some coffee.

It's not fair. I shouldn't be thinking about him like this. We're about to go our separate ways. I'll not see him again. Let's not forget that when he finds out I've been lying to him this entire time, he's going to think worse of me than he does Jasmine.

That hurt. She actually liked Declan and that wasn't even including his prowess in bed. Or along a wall, in the shower, on a couch or any of the other numerous places where he'd taken her to the heights of ecstasy.

Toughen up, Caro. This isn't about you but keeping Jasmine safe.

Okay, so her brain had a point. Her sister was the only reason she'd done this. Nothing more, nothing less. She'd wanted to help her twin.

Where did that get me?

She didn't want to focus on that answer. It had to do with the man confidentially flying the jet. His dedication and sacrifices for her… Dare she even think the word?

No. I refuse to think of that L-word. She wasn't a flighty woman. She didn't believe in love at first sight. And she wasn't willing to accept her feelings toward him. Not in the slightest.

Lie all you want, Caro. You know the truth. At her brain's unwanted commentary, she shut her eyes blocking out the broad shoulders of the man she couldn't stop thinking about. None of it mattered. Eyes open or shut, she could pull up a perfect visual of him.

They talked on the way back about a few random things. She kept him full of coffee and even took over, with it on autopilot, while he went for a quick trip to the bathroom.

He picked up the headset once he returned and put it on his head. When he called the Atlanta tower, she sat up a bit more.

"Patch me through to Detective Lance Baldwin."

I thought that's the man he didn't like and the one I apparently propositioned. Why is he calling him? She angled herself a bit more to see him better. The lights gleamed off his stubbled jaw. He looked drawn and exhausted yet all too hot for her own good.

"Baldwin? McBride. I need your help. Yes, I heard about Daniels."

Wonder if that's the man who died with the other witness.
She rubbed her palms along the seams of her jeans.

"I need you to meet me." A pause. "I'm not sure."

Caro didn't understand what they were saying. One, she didn't know the area so places meant nothing to her. Two, she truly was just so exhausted. She allowed her lids to drift down again. She drifted between sleep and awareness the remainder of their flight.

"November Three-Six-One-Two requesting permission to land."

She woke fully at his words.

The sun had barely begun to creep over the horizon as he lined them up and set them down on the dry tarmac. A black SUV raced toward them and she slanted her gaze to him. Declan didn't seem the least bit worried so she resolved to be calm as well.

She followed him from the cockpit after he'd powered down the jet. Shrugging into her coat, she watched him open the door and lower the steps. He beckoned to her.

"Let's go."

And we're back to the two word communication. She didn't argue, just led the way down. At the bottom she recognized the detective leaning against the running vehicle. The men looked at one another and gave sharp nods but that was it.

She rolled her eyes and climbed in the back. Head against the rest, she shut her eyes and sighed heavily. *Almost over. Then I can go home and get back to my life.*

* * * *

"Let's go."

Caro stirred at those two words. She'd fallen asleep and yawned as they stepped from the SUV in front of a hotel. One cop on each side they walked in and bypassed the desk heading straight for the elevator bay.

She crossed her arms and kept her head down as they rode up. Detective Baldwin stepped out first then gave a jerk of his head, she followed and Declan brought up the rear. They entered a suite and Caro kept her stare down at the floor.

"I'll be back to take you to the courthouse. You have five hours." Baldwin looked at her, ran his gaze over her then left.

Declan locked the door behind Baldwin and leaned against it as he stared at her. "He brought you a suit — it's hanging in the room. Go shower, sleep or whatever you want." He shifted his stance. "No phone calls and no leaving the room."

"Okay."

She turned to the bedroom and walked in its direction before pausing. She chewed the inside of her cheek as she slowly faced him again. Declan McBride. Cop. He stood there, powerful and sure. He'd been through hell — so had she — and still looked ready to take on the world.

"Thank you. For keeping me safe."

Indescribable emotions flashed across his face. "Doing my job."

The words cut her deep. *Guess we're back to the part where we hate one another.* "I know. I was just a job. I get it." She forced a small smile. "Still, you didn't let me die." She walked away from him and into the bathroom, the door closing behind her with a definitive click.

Declan stared after her. *Shit!* He didn't know what to do. He had to do his job and that didn't entail fucking the woman he was supposed to protect. His sore body yelled at him. How was she feeling?

They'd been through hell this past day. She'd been burnt, taken, cut, in a car accident, shot at and more.

Nothing at all how I thought she would have responded to any adversity. I always thought she was selfish. The woman I spent time with was anything but.

He strode to the shut door before he had even thought twice about it and let himself in. The shower ran and he shucked his clothing before stepping into the bathroom. He moved the curtain back and joined the woman he couldn't get enough of under the warm spray.

"What are you doing in here?" Her question was rife with tension and bite. "I know fucking me now isn't part of your job."

He turned her so they were face to face. "Nope, it isn't. I'm here because I want you."

Her response was to reach up and around his neck, drawing him in for a kiss. It wasn't furious or dominating, no—tentative and gentle. His insides turned over and he ignored the soft feelings that grew for her by the second.

"Are you okay?" he asked against her lips.

"Sore. Hand hurts and the cut stings but yeah, I'm okay. You? How's your head?"

Declan reached for a washcloth and soaped it up. "I'll live." He angled her so the spray hit her front while he washed her back. Swipe after slow swipe until he crouched and moved the cloth over the firm globes of her ass then down the backs of her thighs. He washed her feet then stood before rotating her so her back was in the water and rinsed clean.

He wrung out the white cloth and lathered it again. Declan started on her left arm, taking care to avoid the cut, then moved to her right. There, he was careful with the burn on her hand. She stood still, watching his face as he continued to wash her body. Her breasts, stomach, the fronts of her legs. Then he moved on to her pussy. Guiding her legs to widen a bit, he took his time there. The way her breathing changed and her pupils dilated told him she wanted him. As much as he did her.

Ignoring his desire for the moment, he rinsed off her front before starting on her hair. He'd never washed a woman's hair before. The hotel had supplied a stress relief aromatherapy scent. Eucalyptus and spearmint. He lathered it into her hair noting the small mewls she made as he worked his fingers through her locks.

He washed it twice before doing the same thing with the conditioner. Each moan from her was like another layer of iron around his cock.

"You're good at this." She looked at him and wrung out some of the water from her hair. "My turn."

Declan didn't speak as she returned the favor. Her fingers trailed over his skin as she washed him, her touch gentle where needed and firm in other places. She also washed his hair and conditioned it.

"You need to get this looked at," she said brushing along his head wound.

"Later." He reached past her and shut off the water. Without a word, he lifted her, and she wrapped her legs around his waist, her pussy right against his cock. He strode from the bathroom, stopped to grab a condom from his wallet and carried her to the bed.

He covered her with his body and placed the head of his cock at the entrance to her slick pussy. She watched him with large eyes.

"One more time?" Caro's voice was soft and almost unsure.

He nodded and pulled away to sheathe himself. Then he returned to her body and surged inside her with one stroke.

"Ohh, Declan."

He had to hold still for a moment or he'd embarrass himself. Like the first time only better. He knew her body now. Knew how to make it sing. How to make her scream aloud with pleasure. Knew how she affected him and made him roar to the room when he came with a rush.

Staring at her, he continued to wait before moving. She held his gaze. In the depths of her eyes passion swirled. Declan began to move. Their eyes welded on one another as he thrust. He lost himself in the wealth of her silken chocolate irises.

She gripped him tight with her uninjured hand and undulated beneath him. He pressed his lips to hers as he moved. Her body, clean and perfect, rubbing against him was a siren's call to lose control. With an iron will he didn't know he possessed, Declan resisted.

"Faster." Her word was mumbled by the pressure of his lips upon hers.

He shook his head and grabbed her hips, halting her attempt to pick up the pace. His final time with her would not be rushed. He ignored the fact that he was ready to come now and focused on drawing out their time together.

Short strokes to long. Slow thrusts to fast. Their breaths mingled as they moved in tandem. Caro held him tight. She bowed and came with a keening cry.

One. Two. Three. And one more stroke before he shot thick ropes of cum. Limbs weak, he lowered himself carefully to her. She didn't release him or lessen her grip on him.

He kissed the side of her neck and withdrew from her heat. In the bathroom he cleaned himself up. Padding naked back to the bedroom, he paused by the doorframe.

Caro lay on her side, injured arm out and burned hand open by her chin. She slept—soundly from the small snores she emitted.

Declan allowed himself the chance to watch her. Memorize her features. He knew logically that they had no chance now that they were back here in Atlanta. He wasn't a fan of that but there was no reason in thinking on something that couldn't be.

He took a quick shower and dressed. Caro still slept as he closed the bedroom door behind him. He fixed himself some coffee and turned the television on low. The knock at the door had him holding his pistol as he went to check who it was.

Lance Baldwin stood there. Declan swung the door open and locked it again behind the man.

"Where is she?"

"She was sleeping in the bedroom. Not sure if she's awake now."

Lance merely grunted and took a seat. "What happened to your head?"

"Cut it when we went over the edge out there. The vehicle rolled."

"Need a doctor?"

He sat. "Nope. I've been keeping it cleaned. Once I hand her over to the ADA I'll go get checked out. I'm sure LT will holler at me about it."

"What about her? I saw she was bruised as well."

"Like I mentioned to you, it wasn't an easy trip back." He shifted in the seat. "What'd you find out about Jimmy Harstone?"

"He was your link for sure. We ran his name and came up with nothing. But when we ran his picture, the current one you sent, a lot more popped up." He slid a folder across the small table toward Declan. "He's been in Atlanta a lot. Drug problems and many mistresses. He was also a runner for the family."

"So how'd he get into this?"

"Apparently, he wanted back in the good graces of the family. When he heard they were looking for Jasmine, he offered up his knowledge of her being there." He arched an eyebrow. "That includes her using the name Caro."

Declan shrugged. "Not sure why she picked that name. All I know is she answered it a lot better than I would have expected her too."

"Why? Jasmine has numerous aliases."

"I know but none of them were Caro."

"Con artist is a con artist."

He checked the time and noted how long they had. "I'll be right back, gonna make sure she's getting up." Declan wanted to smack the smirk on Lance's face but ignored it, walked to the bedroom door and knocked. "Jasmine. Time to wake up and get ready." He cracked it open and peeked in.

She sat with the blankets captured around her breasts and stared at him through sleepy eyes. "I'll be right there."

Damn it, he wanted to go to her and hold her. Kiss her. "See you don't keep us waiting."

"Us?"

More irrational jealousy hit him. "Detective Baldwin is here as well."

"How nice."

Declan shut the door and went back to his seat. Lance watched him, amusement dancing in his gaze.

They sat in silence for a bit. "She gets to you."

"Not much in the way of approving of her life choices."

"Is that it or the fact she propositioned me?"

Anger churned. "Why would that bother me? My job is to keep her safe, not keep track of her bed partners."

"That's good to know."

He turned at her words and saw her standing there. The hurt that had existed vanished behind a mask of indifference. The dark blue skirt suit molded to her body in ways he wanted to. Up close and personal.

"Ms Hoyer," Baldwin said, standing. "Good to see you again."

"Detective." She turned cool eyes back to him. "Are we leaving or what?"

Cold all the way around. Yep, this was the Jasmine he recalled. His own attitude slipping, he shoved to his feet and rocked back on his heels. "Been waiting on you."

"Didn't know I was supposed to sleep in this outfit and roll out of bed ready to go. Sorry, wasn't aware this was a soap opera." She walked to the door and he had to hurry to beat her there.

He slammed his hand over the door when she went to open it. "You don't need to go first."

"So go and I'll follow if you don't get blown away."

Baldwin chuckled and Declan flipped the man off as he exited the room first. The halls were empty as they made their way to the elevator. She stood silent between the both of them.

Was she closer to Baldwin? Why was he going down this road? *I have got to get it together. What difference does it make if she's closer to him or not? My job, my only job is to keep her alive to the courthouse.*

He slanted his gaze to her and found she stared straight ahead, expressionless. Copying her, he focused on the steel gray doors and waited for them to open. When they did, both men were standing in front of her, blocking her just in case. The hotel was quiet and, after sharing a look with Lance, they headed for the back where he had a vehicle waiting.

Chapter Eleven

Caro blew out a breath as she sat in the back of the unmarked sedan. Both men were in the front so she could stare at them without anyone being the wiser. Although, she did have to be careful, for Detective Baldwin would occasionally check the rear-view and she made sure not to be staring like a lovelorn fool at Declan when that happened.

She flexed her hand and fought the wince. It still hurt where she had burned it on the kettle. *Lord, that seems like such a long time ago instead of yesterday morning. All the shit I've gone through since then.* Unbidden her gaze drifted back to the man in the passenger seat in front of her. Declan McBride.

He hadn't shaved and she didn't mind. Rugged. Handsome. Capable. He had some bruises on his face and the cut on his temple still made her heart hitch.

When I think we could have gone over that mountain and died... I don't know how I'll ever be able to repay him. That was the thing. Her repaying him was going to be informing him that she wasn't Jasmine and hadn't ever been. That he'd risked his life protecting someone else.

The big knot in her chest got larger and she rubbed the spot that rested beneath the white blouse. Baldwin was watching her again and she merely lifted an eyebrow and stared back at him. She didn't miss the slight turn of his lips before he put his attention back on the road. The interior was silent except for the radio echoing with all the calls.

She flexed her fingers and hoped to God her sister would be there. Caro had called again this morning from the bedroom after Declan had told her to get ready. Jasmine had promised she'd be there but Caro wasn't ready to be confident about that until she actually laid eyes upon her. She'd also told her to wear something nice.

Caro moved again and this time Declan looked back at her. His eyebrow cocked as if asking if she were okay. But he didn't vocalize anything so she didn't speak in return. Merely turned away from him. From her periphery she could see him shaking his head.

They pulled up in front of the courthouse and the men climbed out. She allowed herself one more ogle of Declan McBride. His jeans fitted him like a second skin and his shirt only highlighted his powerful muscles. As she sat there, he swung off his coat.

Detective Baldwin opened her door and offered her a hand. She took it and allowed him to assist her to the sidewalk.

"Thank you."

"You're welcome. Thank you for not running away and for testifying."

Yeah, I'm not the one you want. She scanned the steps looking for her sister. Nothing.

"Let's get her inside." Declan's tone was cold and sharp, much like the wind that blew around her.

"You got this, McBride, or do you need some help?"

"I'm fine, Baldwin. Thanks for the help."

"No problem. Let me know when you're ready to become a detective."

Declan's snort wasn't pleasant, and she recalled what he'd told her about his ex. Not just a bitch of a woman but one she was about to go face. Sourness spread and she cleared her throat as they made their way up the steps.

"I need to tell you something," she muttered.

"What now, Jasmine?"

His tone was unbending and irritated, enough that it spiked her own irritation. So much for trying to protect him from the revelation.

"Nothing," she snapped.

The woman who stepped from behind a pillar was the ADA, Jacquelyn Ashcraft. Cold. Professional. Bitch. She wore a power suit and stared down her nose at both of them.

Caro's indignation segued from Declan to his ex-wife. Who the fuck was this woman to look at the two of them like they were shit on the bottom of her shoe?

"You're almost late," she said. Her tone as chilly as her expression.

"Almost isn't late, Jackie." Declan reached out and beckoned Caro closer. "And good to see you again as well. You're welcome for me not letting her die."

The cold gaze found her. "You ready for this?"

"No."

"No?" The woman stepped closer. "What do you mean no?"

"What's hard to understand? Why would I be ready for this? Everyone else who was supposed to testify is dead. I should be looking forward to it with an excitement that rivals a party?" She narrowed her gaze. "Back off."

"You're just like your file. So long as you don't fuck up on the stand."

She peered past her and couldn't even begin to explain the relief that coursed through her. "I hate to disappoint you but I'm not Jasmine."

"Christ, not this again." Declan's words didn't even bother her, she had expected them.

"What do you mean?"

"I mean, my name is Caro. Jasmine is over there." She beckoned to her twin who walked up and took off the large hat she'd been wearing. "She's my twin."

"Are you fucking kidding me?"

Oh, he was pissed off. Caro turned to look at him. Fury emanated from him in waves.

"I think we need to take this inside before it gets louder." The ADA ushered them into a small room.

"Are you okay?" Jasmine asked her, handing over her bag.

"I will be. You?"

"Yes."

Caro squeezed her hand. "You make sure you stay safe. I'm sorry I lost your bag."

"You're safe, that's all I care about."

"Someone want to explain to me what the fuck is going on here?" Jacquelyn dropped her attaché on the table and put her hands on her hips.

Declan grabbed Caro and spun her to him. "You lied? You played that you were Jasmine."

She tugged free and matched him glower for glower. "Not true. I told you that first day I wasn't Jasmine. You told me to shut up and not to even try the 'I'm not Jasmine Hoyer' business. So I did. But I told you I wasn't her."

He shoved his hand through his hair. "Christ, woman, do you have any idea what you did?"

"Allowed my twin to be in a place where she felt safe."

"That was my job!" he hollered.

"Right. And look what happened. Shot at, kidnapped, shoved off the mountain road in an SUV. We both have cuts and bruises. She's fine. What's the big deal? She's here. She's going to testify and as you so aptly put it *we'll* never have to see one another again!"

"How did we not know you had a twin?" Jacquelyn questioned Jasmine.

Her twin crossed her arms and sat on the edge of a table. "Not my fault. Every time one of you people come barging in my life something happens. Why would I tell you anything, especially when you already think you know everything about me?" Jasmine's tone fell bitter and unforgiving.

Caro went to her side and both of them glared at the law in the room. She wouldn't apologize for doing what she could to help her sister.

"I could arrest you," Declan said.

"For what?" Caro bit off. "Telling you I wasn't who you said I was. You're the one who told me who I was, wouldn't even listen to me. Then you kidnapped me and took me to a whole other state where I had to listen to you degrade my character, all because you thought you knew who I was."

"Did you not read that file?" He glared at her.

She stepped close to him. "Couldn't have been all bad if you were willing to fuck me." Her words dripped with derision. "So don't stand there on your high horse, Declan McBride."

"Oh my God, you slept with her? Are you fucking kidding me, McBride?" Jacquelyn screeched. "This is wrong on so many levels."

She glared at the ADA. "Why? I'm not his witness. I'm not your witness. What we did had no bearing on this case."

"He thought you were his witness."

"So he thought wrong. You have the right one here now. And I'm leaving." She whirled back to face her twin whose expression was priceless. "Thanks for keeping my stuff. Stay safe."

She shouldered her pack, pleased that Jasmine had worn something suited for court and they wouldn't have to change outfits. Aside from the pink hair, she looked very pretty. One more hand squeeze and she walked to the door, only to find Declan blocking her way.

"What?" she demanded. Her fingers itched to smack the condescending look from his features.

"You lied to me. You wasted my time trying to keep you safe. If I never see you again, it will be too soon for me."

Ignoring the pain in her heart she sniffed and shot him a look that should have put him six feet under. "And you should learn to listen to people more when they tell you they're not who you assume them to be. You're the one who had the preconception of who I was, wrong though it was."

"Was anything you said true?"

"Does it matter? You have your opinion of me anyway." She stepped to the left to go around him but he moved with her. "Do you mind? I'd just rather get the hell out of here."

"You should be ashamed."

"I should? For what? Fucking you? Trust me, that's becoming more and more of a shame each passing second. For protecting my twin? Never. It worked out in the end. She's here and I'm leaving." This time she shouldered her way by him and slipped out of the door.

It wasn't until she had made it outside and down the steps she noticed there were tears streaming down her face. After flagging down a taxi she jumped inside and wiped her cheeks.

"Where to?" the driver asked.

"Airport, please." She peered in her bag and was grateful to find her cards still there. The cash was gone but at this point she didn't care that Jasmine had used it. She merely wanted to get home and forget the hell she'd just gone through.

"Leaving our city so soon?"

She met his dark gaze in the rear-view. "I have to get back to work. My boss is expecting me. For some reason he doesn't like paying me if I don't do anything."

The man laughed and she managed a small smile.

"Which terminal?"

"Delta." It didn't matter. All that did was that she was able to depart as quickly as possible.

So she did.

* * * *

Declan stood at the back of the courtroom while Jasmine took the stand. Rage flowed freely through him.

Why are you so pissed? his brain asked.

Because she lied to me. She. Caro. Not Jasmine.

How they had missed that Jasmine had a twin he hadn't a clue. However, he knew he needed to go look this up and find out just who Caro was. Part of him was thrilled Caro and Jasmine were two different people.

When Jasmine finished and walked toward him, he made sure to step in front of her before she left the courtroom. He made note of the members of Kazakova's family who were in the galley.

"We need to talk."

"Come to apologize for fucking my sister?" she sneered.

He gripped her arm and led her from the room. Catching sight of an empty chamber, he shoved her in there and kicked the door closed behind them. "Tell me who she is."

Her laugh—nothing like Caro's—grated along his nerves. "Fuck you."

He stared at the woman and realized there was nothing about her that drew him to her. The women may look alike but his body recognized the difference in them. And wanted the other one. Not the pink-haired one before him.

"No thanks. Why didn't you mention you had a twin?"

She crossed her arms and sat at the edge of the table. "Why'd you fuck her? Think it was me? Wanted to get some of this?"

He narrowed his gaze. *I won't let her pull me from my goal here.* "Name."

Her grin rubbed him wrong. "Jasmine Hoyer."

"Hers."

She pushed up and walked toward him, hips swaying and her look fully seductive. "Make no mistake, Officer McBride. I don't like you. I don't like any of your brothers in blue. Can't say I shed any tears for the one who died the other day. You and your kind mean shit to me. We both know the only reason I'm testifying is to get a reduced sentence on the drug charges your ADA leveled against me. It's a big reduction."

Jasmine stared briefly at her sky blue nails. "I'm not scared of Jacquelyn Ashcraft or the Kazakova crime family. Nor am I scared of you. I live for my drugs and that's about it. The only other thing I give a damn about is my twin. I'm a cold heartless bitch but I love my sister. So make no mistake when I say you can go fuck yourself and take your intimidation tactics with you. I. Don't. Care."

"Then how did you get her to help you? And why risk her?"

"I knew you'd keep her safe. Didn't know you'd fuck her but I knew she'd be safe with you. I had to get my new digs set up. I have to disappear after this. I'm not a fool. You may think so but I'm not. I was free to do that while she was with you. They spent all their time trying to figure out where you'd taken her—I was able to move around."

"What's up with you and Jimmy Harstone?"

"That fucker? We used to do drugs and fuck when he'd come to town. Why?"

"He was the one who sold out your sister."

Darkness swirled in her gaze. "Did he hurt her?"

"Nothing more than superficial wounds. He thought she was you. Wanted to rekindle your relationship."

"What happened?"

"She beaned him in the head with a tree branch and knocked him out."

"Good."

There was a knock on the door and Jacquelyn walked through. Declan turned to look at his ex. She wasn't in a good mood.

"Well?" he asked.

"It's going to take a bit longer," she replied. "The judge listened to the defense lawyer and is granting them a bit more time."

Jasmine walked toward her. "Is this your way of trying to renege on our deal?"

"You have to see this through, Ms Hoyer, or there is no deal."

"Wouldn't it just suck if I got amnesia?" She circled her like a wolf circling its prey. "Don't try to fuck with me on this." Without another word, Jasmine left, shutting the door behind her.

Declan glanced at his watch and headed for the door.

"Where are you going?" she asked.

"Leaving. I have to report in to LT and get my head wound checked out. I'm fine, by the way, thanks for asking. Besides, shouldn't you be heading after your witness to make sure they don't gun her down in open space?"

"You're supposed to be protecting her."

"Nope. My job was to get her here to the courthouse. She was here." He stepped out, walked away from her cussing. Declan continued on out the front where LT waited for him, sitting on the hood of his Crown Vic.

"You don't look too worse for the wear."

"Thanks, LT." He climbed in the passenger seat.

"Hospital?"

"You'll take me anyway if I say no, why bother asking?"

"Giving you a chance to prove you've grown up."

"Just drive."

They left the courthouse and he closed his eyes. *I need some sleep. Uninterrupted sleep.*

* * * *

After the hospital, LT drove him home. He waved to his lieutenant and trudged up the steps to his apartment, grabbing his mail along the way.

Once he'd closed the door behind him, he beelined for the bedroom, dropping the mail on the table. He stripped down and stepped into his shower, turning the water on as hot as he could handle it.

He let it work out the knots and remaining kinks he had. Declan didn't tarry and he walked out to wrap a towel around his waist. He dried off and tossed the towel on the chair by his bed, seconds before he climbed in and shut his eyes.

The incessant ringing of his doorbell woke him. Yawning, he rolled from his bed and searched for some sweatpants that he slipped into. He opened the door and frowned.

"What are you doing here, and what do you want?"

Jacquelyn Ashcraft brushed by him as if she had every right to be in his place. "I brought you food. We need to talk."

Her blonde hair drawn back in a tight bun emphasized her cheekbones. He slammed the door after her. "About what? Christ, Jackie, I was sleeping."

"Don't call me Jackie."

He rolled his eyes. The woman could be dying and that response would slip out to anyone who called her anything other than Jacquelyn Ashcraft or Ms Ashcraft. He scratched his chest and went after her. She pulled down plates and cups with a disturbing familiarity.

He didn't help, just sat after getting himself a cup of Joe. "What's so important you had to come down here? Don't you live more uptown?"

"You know very well where I live, McBride. No need to be an ass. Are you going to help me?"

"Nope." He drank some coffee. "You came barging in here bringing food. You serve it."

"Ass."

He sniffed. He'd been called much worse. "Clock's ticking, Jackie."

She slammed a bowl before him with curried chicken and rice in it. "Stop calling me that."

"You can live where you want and dress in your expensive clothes, but you're still Jackie to me."

"I'm nothing to you. We're no longer married."

"I'm aware of that. Grateful as well." He shoveled in some food and his belly grumbled in anticipation.

"You're more of an ass now than when we were married."

He lifted an eyebrow. "Is that even possible? According to you there wasn't a bigger ass than I was then."

"Christ. I didn't come for this. We have to talk about your witness."

He laughed and drank some more coffee. "She's not my anything."

Her green eyes narrowed. "You fucked her."

"I fucked Caro. Not Jasmine." Just thinking about her had him hardening in his sweats. And he was grateful the table kept that knowledge from his ex.

"You thought it was Jasmine."

"Is this what you came to discuss? My sleeping habits?" He ate some more. "I never knew you cared so much."

"I want that other woman back here."

"Caro?"

"Whatever. Bring her here. I think Jasmine will be more cooperative if her sister is near."

More laughter spilled from him. "I'm not your personal assistant. Besides, I don't know where the hell this woman lives." He swirled his coffee in his mug. "You want her here, I suggest you go find her."

"I'm the ADA."

He narrowed his gaze. "And I'm just a lowly cop, right? So whatever I must have to do can't possibly be as important. Lovely as always to be in your presence, Jackie. Leave my house."

"You could be so much more than just a cop, Declan."

"Just a cop? You do know, Jackie, that it's not only detectives who solve cases, right? Cops do that as well. We also have paperwork to file and get this—we talk to people as well. Not just the detectives."

"You have so much potential."

"I'm happy where I am. And you've already made it perfectly clear that a cop's not good enough for you so go get one of your esteemed detectives to be your errand bitch. I have streets to protect." He nodded at the door. "Bye."

"I can order you—"

"I don't work for you. Never have. Never will. Get out of my place, Jackie, before I toss you out on your ass. I'm done with this case. Don't come to me, don't assume I will help. Leave me out of it. Remember, I'm just a cop."

"Asshole."

She stomped away. He didn't even flinch when the door slammed behind her. After finishing up his food, he went back to bed. This time, however, it was visions of Caro that accompanied him.

Chapter Twelve

Terri brought her another hot toddie and curled up beside her on the sofa. Caro scratched at the gauze around her hand and sighed.

"So, tell me more. What was his name?"

"McBride. Declan McBride."

Her friend grinned. "Sounds hot. What's he do?"

"He's a cop with Atlanta PD."

"A cop? How'd you meet him?"

"He's the one who saved me from all of this." She gestured at her body.

Terri sobered. "Are you sure you don't want to go to the hospital?"

"I'm sure. I just need to relax a bit. I called my parents and told them I was back. And I said I'd see them in a few days. I don't think I could handle my mom's inquiry right now. Besides, I also need to tell them about Jasmine."

Terri squeezed her hand. "It will work out. Now, tell me more about this cop." She shook her head. "I can't believe he took you all the way to California."

"He didn't think it was me, remember?"

"Right. She could have put you in a lot of trouble."

"I know. But as much as I'd like to blame her for that, I'm the one who agreed to continue going along with it. I'm as much to blame as she is."

"You're much too good of a person, Caro. I would have beat her for pulling what she did."

"She's not had it easy, Terri."

"So what? That's not your fault. At all. Stop trying to think you need to feel guilty because you had a good life growing up."

"We're twins."

"Apparently a good one and a bad one."

Caro didn't take offense. Terri was a psychiatrist and didn't pull punches with her opinions. One of the reasons they got along so well. She nodded. "I know. But she came back and showed up in the end."

"After taking your money and having access to your credit cards." She gave a pointed look. "Did you take care of that?"

"I did. I'm ignoring the money, I don't care about that. But yes, I'm having all my cards changed."

"Good."

"Now. Enough about her. I want to know what this man was like in bed."

Heat surged through her making her wonder if she hadn't just imagined the snow that fell outside her window and that they were truly on a beach in the Caribbean. Terri pointed at her and laughed.

"I can see your reaction from here. Christ, was he that good?"

"Better."

"Damnation. Does he have a brother?"

"I don't know. There's another cop, well, detective actually, who was hot as well. His name was Detective Lance Baldwin."

"Lance. That's a good strong name. Wonder what the size of his lance is."

"You're so bad."

"I'm horny."

She held up her hands. "Don't look in this direction. I'm there for you for just about anything but that. You're on your own."

Terri harrumphed.

"I'll spring for some batteries, though, that's about as far as I'll go in my contribution to the cause."

"I may take you up on that."

They toasted and sat in silence while they drank, listening to the fire crackle in the fireplace and relaxing. Caro couldn't explain how glad she was to be home. She had taken a long hot bath in her tub, just lying there allowing the heat to permeate her bones and make her feel a bit more human. Then she'd called Terri. Had cried it all out, eaten, and now here they were.

"Will you see him again?" Terri broke the quiet.

Caro turned her head to stare at her best friend. "For what reason?" She placed the empty mug beside her and got up to tend the fire.

"I don't know. A good humping."

She snorted. "No more watching *Evolution* for you." She added another piece of wood. "Besides, he made it painfully and perfectly clear he'd not be wanting to see me again."

"Are you sure you didn't misunderstand?"

Returning the poker to the stand, Caro nodded. "Positive. He said, and I quote, 'If I never see you again, it will be too soon for me.' So I'm thinking he'll be fine with me staying up here in Wisconsin and not invading his life in Atlanta."

Terri spun the stem of her wine glass and pursed her lips a few times. "Things often said in anger are not true."

"And sometimes they reflect the truest of our emotions." She retook her seat. "Look, I get what I did to him was wrong. I had my reasons and I won't make excuses for them. I did what I did and now I have to deal with the repercussions. Am I sad I don't have a chance with him? Yes. Of course I am. He's one hell of a man and I'm not talking just in the bedroom."

"You admire him."

"A hell of a lot more than I thought I would." Adjusting her sock, she looked at her friend. "Jasmine's file is"—she shook her head—"reading I won't soon forget, let's put it that way. Yet, despite all she'd done to him and the ones who wear the uniform, he never hesitated to put himself in danger to keep her, or rather me, safe. That's impressive. Then he saved my life more than once on the way back here. I mean, how many people can say their vehicle was pushed over the side of a mountain in winter and talk about it? He took bullets for me."

"This is more than hero worship."

"It's not hero worship, I know that."

Terri's eyebrows rose. "I know it too. You're in love with the man."

Caro blinked and stared at her. "Excuse me?"

"You love this man. It's all over your expression when you talk about him, hell when you think about him. I see the love you have for him."

She closed off her facial features, hiding her emotion and displaying what she knew would be an unreadable mask. Terri laughed then coughed to clear her throat. "Sweetie, you can shutter up all you want but I know the truth."

"I don't know what you're talking about," she denied.

"Of course not," Terri drolled. "What was I thinking? Hmm, if only I did something for a living that allowed me to see past people's bullshit. What's that? I do? Really?"

"You are such a bitch," Caro said.

"You always say that when I'm right and you're not."

Caro snapped her mouth shut. The woman had the right of it. With a shrug she turned her head and stared at the fire.

"I'm not going away, Carolyn."

"I don't want to talk about this."

"Fine. We don't have to, won't change any of the facts. But I'm not your doc. At least not right now. You keep denying yourself and you may be coming to see me."

Caro peered at her friend. "You write prescriptions for batteries?"

Terri laughed. "Not for anyone but you, darling."

The timer went off indicating their dinner was ready and they walked to the kitchen. Terri pulled out the salad while Caro grabbed the main course from the broiler. Her palm stung and she shook her head over the lingering pain from the burn. She hated feeling less than one hundred percent.

They ate their main then enjoyed some dessert, toasted coconut cake, which Terri had brought with her. Until late in the night, they chatted about anything and everything. When Terri left, Caro hugged her and watched her go across the hall to her apartment. A final wave and she locked her own door then walked back to the fire and sat before it. Unable to hold still, she moved to the large window that overlooked her city. Bracing against the wall next to it, she stared out as more snow blanketed the streets. They were having an unusually high snowfall this year. She didn't mind.

"Only one thing could make this better."

Declan.

She shook her head at her brain's commentary and closed the curtains before making her way to her bedroom. After ensuring to set her alarm, Caro climbed between the sheets and shut off the light. Sleep eluded her for a while as she couldn't find a way to get images of Declan McBride out of her mind.

Her rest had been fitful at best when she woke. She got ready for work and walked down with Terri beside her.

"Dinner out tonight?" Terri asked as they paused by their vehicles.

"I think that would be wonderful. Where do you want to meet?"

"Buck & Badger work?"

"Haven't been there for a while, sounds good to me. It'll be good to be back there."

"About seven? Or don't you think you'll be done with work by then."

"Shoot, for Buck & Badger I'll be done by five if you want to meet then. When's your last patient?"

"Five it is. Don't worry, I'll be there."

She opened the door to her Outback and nodded. "See you then."

"Bye, hon. Be good." Terri waved and ducked into her BMW.

Adjusting her music, Caro followed her friend from their parking garage and waved as she went toward campus while her friend went in the other direction.

* * * *

Declan swore and punched the bag hanging before him with three more rapid strikes. He was in a mood. And not a pleasant one. After a few more punches he looked up to see his lieutenant crossing the gym floor. He wiped the back of his hand along his brow. The wrap around his hands was a bit scratchy but nothing major when it hit the lingering head injury.

Despite his desire to keep punching, he waited, well aware LT was coming over to him. He hitched up his low slung sweats and stood.

"McBride."

"What's up, LT?"

"Why is the ADA calling my office?"

He shrugged. "Beats me. Did you ask them?"

"Not in the mood, McBride."

Neither was he, yet somehow he assumed that wouldn't matter. He crossed his arms.

"That bitch, Ashcraft. Left me ten—got that—*ten* messages." He paced. "Like I have nothing else to do but her bidding."

Although he had an idea why, Declan still posed the question, "What does this have to do with me?"

"She wants you to talk to Jasmine Hoyer. Guess she's not cooperating well."

He shook his head. "Not my case, LT. I've got plenty of my own work stacked up on my plate."

"I heard what happened. With the twin."

He held his lieutenant's gaze. "Point being?"

"Just I know it's not easy being duped."

Declan refused to go down that road. He'd shut the door and had no desire—no intention—of going back through it.

"Let me make this clear, LT. I've done my job. I'm not at her beck and call. I'm no longer married to her and I *refuse* to be pushed into doing work for her. She thinks uniforms are shit anyway and detectives are so damn special, like I told her, get them to do it."

"You know the DA will step in."

"Still not sure why that concerns me. DA isn't my boss. Perhaps she should thaw out and be human."

"Always have to make this personal, McBride?" LT played with his pack of cigarettes.

He looked over to see Jackie approaching, a familiar scowl upon her lips. Dismissing her without a word he picked up his towel and tossed it over his shoulder.

"Anything else, LT?"

"Nope."

His lieutenant was good people. And he wasn't any more of a Jackie fan than Declan.

"I'm trying to talk to you, McBride." Her tone was icy.

"Sounds like you should be talking to your witness. I have to get ready for my shift."

Declan walked away and into the men's room. In the shower he swore as he washed his hair when he saw his ex-wife pause by the stall.

"Did you think walking into a bathroom would stop me?"

He groaned. *Can't this woman just leave me alone?*

"What are you doing?"

He rolled his eyes. "Jacking off and trying to tune you out. What the fuck do you think I'm doing in the shower before my shift?" Declan tipped his head down and rinsed. "Leave, Jackie. I'm not doing your job."

"It's Jacquelyn. What about the officer that died?"

"What about him? You know who killed him?"

"No, but we're sure it's—"

"The Kazakova family. I know. But you don't know who actually did the killing so why are you trying to use that?"

"Damn it! Can't you just help out?"

He shut off the shower and used his towel before wrapping it around his waist. Then he left the stall.

Jackie ran a critical gaze over him but he felt nothing. Hand on the towel he walked to his locker. A few other officers in there stared unabashedly between him and the woman trailing behind him.

"You have an obligation, McBride."

He faced her. "My obligation? My job is not yours to control. You aren't my chief, deputy chief, or my LT. Do not tell me what my obligations are. You want Caro, go find her yourself. Talk to your witness—perhaps she knows where her twin is. Either way, leave me out of it."

Declan opened the door and withdrew his uniform. Tilting his head in her direction, he raised an eyebrow. "Staying for a show?"

"I've already seen it, remember? I walked away."

Chuckles and snickers came from the others. He didn't mind. She'd long since been able to embarrass him.

"Staying now. Looking for a refresher?" He faced her fully. "I charge for shows and despite our history that goes even for you."

She glared then whirled around on her expensive heels before she stomped away. At the door, she paused to glare once more at him before departing the locker room.

Declan ignored the ribbing and dressed. Hooking on his duty belt, he laughed along with some of the raunchy jokes being told. He double-checked his boots then grabbed his cap and left to attend his briefing.

* * * *

"Stop! Police!" Declan yelled as he ran after his suspect.

Feet pounding, he called in his position as they ran into an alley. Ahead, the young man scrambled up the chain link fence. Cursing, Declan turned on his speed and yanked him down to the ground.

"I'm innocent!"

"Shut up," he barked.

He rolled him over and cuffed him.

"What did I do, man?"

Declan read him his rights and hauled him to his feet. "Why'd you run if you didn't do anything?" If the man wasn't going to be quiet, he may as well ask questions.

"You're a cop and were chasing me."

"Hadn't thought that running would make you even more guilty-looking?"

"Dude, look at me. You're a white cop. I'm Mexican."

He rolled his eyes. "Really? I hadn't noticed."

"Why wouldn't I run?"

They left the alley and turned back up toward his squad car.

"Because, according to you, you're claiming innocence. Running makes you look guilty."

"I am innocent, man."

"Sure you are." He reached in the man's pocket and pulled out the wallet then flipped it open. "According to this, you're a black woman named Karley."

"My girlfriend."

He grunted. "Uh-huh. That's why when you took it she was screaming you were a thief." He pushed him forward and called in the collar.

After he had gotten him into the back of his squad car, Declan filled out an incident report and gave his card with the case number on it to the woman. Another car rolled up and he passed the perp over, finished what he needed to and got back to it.

By the end of his shift he was sore. It had been a day chock full of chases and tackles. Uncommon typically but today had been odd all the way around starting with Jackie coming into the locker room. Like most days he'd been working full and long days, even accepting extra shifts. Bottom line he was keeping himself too busy to think of anything but the job. How he wanted it. He had picked to work in the downtown area of the city for a reason. If all he had were jaywalkers, he wouldn't feel as if he made any real contribution.

He became a cop to make a difference. He would go anywhere in this city, if needed. He had a rep, hard but fair.

Back at the station, he hefted his bag and walked inside. At his desk he sat to do his paperwork. He hurried through it, wanting to get home and do something other than obsess over the woman he'd not see again.

So I could have handled it better when I found out she'd lied. Sue me. I'm human. I tend to react harshly for some things.

Declan finished up and nodded to some of the officers just coming on shift. He stood and put his bag on his desk. Rooting around in it, he found what he was looking for then zipped it back up when his phone rang.

Shit. He was off duty. Shaking his head, he reached for it. "Officer McBride."

"We need to talk."

Jackie. "Nope. I'm off the clock. Night, Jackie." He hung up and walked out before she could get another word in edgewise.

Declan walked to his truck and, after opening the door, tossed the bag across the front seat. Following it in, he started the engine and with a wave to a few others, he pulled out and headed home.

Once there, he showered, then changed and stood in the kitchen waiting for his microwave dinner to finish heating up. That in hand, he went to settle in and watch a bit of Sportscenter.

That was his routine for the next week. One night he dozed on the couch and the phone woke him. With a yawn he checked the clock. Midnight. Reaching for the receiver he sat up.

"Hello?"

"McBride? It's Dawson down at dispatch."

"What's up, man?"

"Sorry to bother you but a woman's been calling for you. A Terri Mosse."

Name didn't ring a bell to him. "Did she say what it was in regards to?"

"Nope but she's called five times looking for Officer McBride. She's on hold now."

"Patch her through. Thanks, Dawson."

"Sure thing."

"Officer McBride," he said when the call clicked.

"Officer Declan McBride?"

"Yes, ma'am. What can I do for you?"

"I'm sorry to call you late but I don't know who else to try."

"I'm not following."

"Three Russians came in, kicked in her apartment door and took her."

A slither skated up his spine. "Took who?"

"Caro. The one who posed as her twin, Jasmine. Look, I know you don't know me from a hole in the ground. I'm her best friend, she told me about you when she got back. But tonight I heard a commotion and saw them take her."

Ice filled his veins. "Where are you?"

"Wisconsin."

Fuck! How'd they find her up there? *Why didn't you?* his brain countered. He ignored that—now wasn't the time he needed to have a crisis of conscience.

"How do you know they were Russians? Did you call the cops up there and what did they say?"

"I speak Russian, my boyfriend is from there. I did call them. They brushed me off. And those three who took her said something about holding her for leverage to get Kazakova out."

He bolted upright and headed for the door before he had realized what he was doing. "Fuck."

"Look, I don't know much about you but she trusted you. The cops up here will look here but I'm guessing this has to do with what she went to Atlanta to help her crazy twin with. So that's in your jurisdiction. Can you help me? Will you help me? Help me get her back."

Chapter Thirteen

Caro stirred and tried to move. Nothing. She hurt. Much like she had after the car had gone over the side in the mountains. That kind of hurt. Flashes of what she'd endured smashed through her and she tried, unsuccessfully, to make sense of it all.

They'd broken into her apartment, shattering the door as though it'd been constructed from toothpicks. She hadn't understood what they had yelled at her but she knew it was Russian. Terri's long-time boyfriend spoke it all the time with Terri and his family.

Of the three men, the largest had backhanded her sending her careening over the end table and couch to hit the floor. She'd tried to run. Tried to scream. Nothing had worked. She'd been hit a few more times before they'd thrown a bag over her head and someone had carried her over their shoulder.

Now she sat tied to a chair. She couldn't see anything because the bag remained. Her fears would be less if it could be off her head. Hopefully. She flexed her fingers wincing at the painful rush of blood surging through them. Her heart thundered and she tried to slow her breathing.

The rank interior of the bag brought tears to her eyes. *Then again it could be the situation. Either way, I have to calm down. Panicking will get me nowhere. I can figure this out.* Her little pep talk didn't help much.

She heaved a heavy sigh. Her chest hurt along with her abdomen. And jaw. *Everything hurts.* Caro tried to move her legs only to discover she couldn't do that either. The ropes cut into her ankles. *Trussed up like a Thanksgiving turkey.*

What did they want from her? Why'd they taken her?

She heard—faintly—the door shut and footsteps near her location.

Swiping her tongue along her lips, hoping for moisture, she waited. It was a failed attempt for soothing the dryness. Her head wobbled when the bag was yanked away. She squinted against the harsh glare of lights. There, before her, stood a large figure — one she couldn't make out.

He gripped her chin painfully and pushed her head back. She struggled to get away but it was impossible. Slowly, his face came into focus. Harsh features covered by short-cropped facial hair. His nose appeared to have been broken a few times in his past. Still a good-looking man.

He had blue eyes that...held no emotion. Dead eyes. More than anything, that scared her. A small bit of emotion would be better than none.

"Who are you?" She forced the question past her busted lip, ignoring its sting. *It feels like I have some loose teeth as well.*

His smile was disturbing on so many levels. She swallowed back the bile threatening to escape. Staring back at him she took in his nice slacks and shirt. *Maybe I should hurl on him.*

"I get you." He gave a leering grin. "This will be fun for me. Not so much for you. No matter. It's fun for me. That's important."

Fear spiked. "Y…you get me? What's that mean?" *Why am I asking this? I don't think it's in my best interest to know.*

He leaned in close and flashed a perfect grin. "It means, lovely, when *he* gets what *he* wants, *I* get what *I* want."

Words that only added to her fear instead of alleviating it. "He? Who's he?"

Now his gaze grew dark with emotion—sadistic glee. *Okay, so I was wrong when I wanted to see emotion in his gaze. I really, really don't.*

"Boss man."

"Am I supposed to know who that is?"

"Mr Kazakova. You know him."

It didn't sound like a question to her but she decided to respond as if it were one. She shook her head. "No, afraid I haven't had the pleasure."

From the look on his face, she didn't want to.

"No matter. I will keep you. We will have fun."

Meaning him. "So you've said. What I don't know is what you want with me?"

"Leverage."

"I don't understand. Leverage for what?" *How come in the movies when people are captured and tied up like this they manage witty banter and look so calm? It's official, I need to stop watching so many movies and get out more.*

"Get him free."

Shit. This is not good. Anyway I try to slice it, all I end up with is a piece of shit pie. Or you've been fucked cake. "And you think holding me will accomplish that?"

"If they don't want you returned to them in pieces."

She gulped. "Oh great." Her tone was an octave higher.

"I don't want to cut you up piece by piece. Body part by body part. It would ruin *our* time together."

It was official. She wanted to puke her guts up.

"Can't have that, can we?"

The door opened, admitting two more men. She recognized them from her apartment. Their looks were even more unsettling. Neither smiled and both glared.

She sat in silence as they conversed amongst themselves. Occasionally they turned their attention to her, piercing her with looks that further unsettled her.

One walked toward her and withdrew a wicked-looking knife. She stiffened as he bent down and sliced through her ropes. "You make trouble, I use this on you."

The ropes fell away and she immediately rubbed and moved her limbs.

Whack!

He backhanded her in the jaw and sent her flying off the chair into the wall with a hard thump. Tears burned her eyes and some spilled free. No one helped her — not that she expected them to.

She made several attempts to get up before giving in and remaining against the wall. The urge to succumb and cry nearly overwhelmed her but she struggled to not give in.

Crying won't do anything. I can do this. She was on her own. Twin or not, she didn't trust Jasmine to assist if that were the case.

She managed to reposition herself upright and maneuvered herself into the corner where she used one wall to support her head. More tears fell as she thought about her parents and how this would affect them.

I never got to say goodbye. Whether or not a deal was made with getting their boss out, she knew they wouldn't let her go.

The idea of never hugging her parents again, or participating in another game night while they munched on homemade doughnuts and wine, was painful to digest—to say the least. This wasn't how she wanted to end her life.

Regrets suck. I won't give up without a fight. I can't. There's too much left for me to do.

"We go." The one who had said that he would keep her walked near. "Get on feet."

Slowly, she did as he'd ordered and as her legs screamed with agony, she went to his side. His strong bruising grip dug into her arm as he dragged her toward the door. The other two flanking them, they pushed outside and she braced herself for the cold that never came.

Where am I? This isn't Wisconsin. No snow covered the ground and she looked around but didn't see much beyond the numerous rows of warehouses. They passed a vehicle as they headed for the car door and she saw the license plate. Georgia. They shoved her in the back and her new keeper slid in after her. The other two got in the front. They pulled left the area and she could see the skyline.

Shit. I'm back in Atlanta. Immediately her thoughts turned to Declan. He was out there somewhere in this city. That alone gave her a sprig of hope, no matter how tiny it may be, she gripped it and held on for dear life. He would find her. He would rescue her.

Right, a man who said if he never saw you again it would be too soon. She ignored that reminder. He was a man of honor and put his career and job before everything else, including personal feelings.

Staring at the skyline as it neared she prayed. Prayed he would find her and get her out of this hell she knew waited for her. They pulled into a different area and drove up a long drive. She stared at the opulent home as they passed it to park. They exited the vehicle and she stood gazing around before her world went black.

* * * *

Declan didn't even bother to hide his scowl as he strode down the mostly quiet halls of the District Attorney's floor. He paused for a brief second then pushed open the door with the name Jacquelyn Ashcraft painted on the frosted glass.

She glared at him from her seat, eyebrows up in surprise.

"Hang up," he ordered.

Jackie held up a finger and turned her chair so he couldn't see her face. He growled low in his throat and pushed down on the base, ending her call. Sparks flew from her eyes when she whipped back to glare at him.

"Dammit, McBride! You have some gall coming in here and ending one of my calls like that."

"They took Caro."

Her eyebrows snapped close together, and she shook her head, momentarily thrown off track. "What are you talking about?"

"Kazakova's men took Caro."

She leaned back in her chair, crossing one toned leg and tapping the end of her pencil on the desk. "What do you want me to do about it?"

He paused then slammed his hands on the desktop, taking satisfaction in seeing her jump. "You are such a bitch, Jackie. For all your high touting shit, you're still just a cold-hearted bitch. Fuck you." He spun around and slammed the door on her as she called after him.

He bypassed the elevator and took the stairs down. Back in his truck, he drummed his fingers on the wheel as he thought about the past eight hours. He'd gotten off the phone with Terri then called the Madison Police Department and had the report sent to him as well as speaking with one of the responding officers. He'd gone to the station, perused what they'd sent him and tried his best to find out more about what was going on. Then he'd gone to see Jackie.

Obviously a mistake. He punched the gas at the green and headed back to the station. After he parked, he strode in and headed straight for LT's office. This time he knocked.

"Come on in, McBride. Shut the door behind you."

He did as ordered and took a seat across from his boss. "Don't bother telling me to let it go, LT. I won't do it."

"I know you won't. That's not what I'm going to tell you. I was going to say is I've arranged for Jasmine to be made available to you, they're bringing her here. And if you want to talk to Kazakova that can be done as well."

"Damn right I want to talk to that fucker."

LT nodded. "Tell me what you know."

Declan did and the man listened throughout the entire thing. When LT had been caught up, Declan leaned back in his chair and rested one ankle on his other leg.

"Did you check flight logs?"

Declan steepled his fingers beneath his chin. "I did. Found a flight which went to Wisconsin and came back early this morning. Like around three thirty it landed. Owned by the Kazakova family."

"So you think she's here."

"I know she is." He couldn't stand the thought of her in their clutches. "All I have to do now is find out where she is and get her out of there."

LT glanced past him and beckoned to someone with a hand gesture. Declan turned around in time to see Detective Baldwin enter the room and shut the door behind him. They exchanged a head nod before Baldwin sat in the seat beside him.

"You're going to need some help, McBride. Don't argue with me on this. You're officially taking some time off so you can find her. Baldwin here will be your backup if you need it. Of course the rest of us are available as well."

Lance turned slightly in the chair. "I know this family. I know a lot about them. I used to be in the gang task force. If she's here, in this city, we'll find her."

Declan tried to calm down but he wanted to be out there. Scouring every inch he could until she was back in his arms. "Did you have someone pick up Jimmy?"

LT drank some coffee. "I did. He'll be here soon. You know the Feds will want in on this."

"Fuck 'em. I'm not sitting around while some pencil pushers want to engage in a jurisdictional pissing match. They better stay out of my way."

LT's smile bordered on feral. "Like I said, you're on leave, McBride. You'll have no reason to interact with them." He leaned back in his chair, leather and springs squeaking. "You should go talk to Kazakova before they arrive."

Both he and Baldwin stood. "Thanks, LT."

"Don't mention it. At all."

"No, sir." Declan faced the door. "Let's go, Baldwin."

They didn't speak as they left. Outside in the bullpen he looked to the man beside him. Baldwin carried himself with an impressive presence. He looked capable and there lived a hint of trouble and danger in his gaze.

"You don't have to come to meet him with me."

"I think I should. I'll stay in the observation room so he doesn't know I'm there but this way I can refute things if he's lying. He shouldn't see me. If they know I'm there they may put her somewhere new. A location I don't know about."

"Meet you there."

"I'll be about five minutes behind you." Baldwin walked off without a look back or another word.

Declan zipped up his jacket as he went to his truck. He ignored everyone and just left. Driving down to where they were holding Kazakova he tried his best not to think about the numerous witnesses who had been killed by this family. Caro would be fine. She had to be.

He went in and asked to speak to the prisoner. Declan watched them escort him into the room. Sacha Kazakova wasn't an impressive man by any means. In fact he was one people could walk by on the street and he wouldn't make any type of impression. He stood five-nine, a bit portly and had a face that didn't stand out. His head of thinning hair only added to the anonymity he possessed.

Declan wasn't fooled. The man was a stone cold killer. Sacha sat across from him and the guard who'd escorted him in left.

"Officer McBride. Something I can do for you?"

"Where is she?"

Blue eyes blinked at him. "You think I have a woman in here with me? Trust me, it would be nice but sadly they don't allow that. I've not had a woman in months. Perhaps you could put in a word so I could get some. I find myself longing for a nice black woman. Fit. Lovely curves. Dark brown hair that falls past her shoulders. A small mole on the base of her spine. No tattoos, though. Know a woman like that?"

He curved his hands into fists at the description of Caro. It took all the control in the world not to punch him in the face. He shrugged. "Sorry, like you said, you can't have one."

He gave a slight smile. "Soon I'm sure she'll be in my reach."

"Where is she?" His question was lower and more gravelly this time.

"I'm sure I don't know what you're discussing, Officer."

Declan narrowed his gaze. "If anything happens to her, I'll come back here and take it out of your ass. Do I make myself clear?"

"Are you threatening me?"

"Nope. That's a promise, pure and simple. I will take everything you love from you, demolish your organization and leave you with nothing but memories."

Sacha's eyes hardened, the first sign of emotion. "Don't threaten me, Officer, when all it takes is one call and I can have you wiped from the face of this earth."

"And one from me will do the same to you. You're not the only one with ties, Kazakova. Think about my name, McBride, and figure it out. I don't play games and I won't stand for you hurting my woman. We both know your men have her. You want something in return. There will be no deals other than this. You want to keep living and breathing air, you return her to me. Unharmed."

Declan sat back unaware he'd leaned in so close to Sacha. The man held his gaze before grinning. The hairs on the back of Declan's neck stood up.

"You are more than what people give you credit for."

"And you're the same as everyone states. Full of your own worth. Tell me where she is."

He splayed his fingers out on the table and stared at his nails. "You want me to make it easy for you?"

"So you do have her."

"We both know the answer to that will never be vocalized. Any other questions?"

"Is she unharmed?"

He sniffed. "She's alive." A wicked grin. "I would assume. Again, Officer, I'm in here. I don't know what goes on out there."

"You're right. So there's no reason for me not to have you put in solitary. No privileges. One hour in the yard alone. Better that way, all around." He leaned closer. "All your little perks, gone. Your life is going to be the hell I decide until she's back."

"Piece by little piece if I am not released."

The words were whispered and chilled him to the bone. Declan didn't allow it to show on his face. Instead he smiled. "Each one of her correlates to one of yours. And since you won't get a chance to pass that message along, you'd better hope your men keep their hands to themselves."

"You talk a good game, McBride. But can you back it up?"

"It's already been arranged. Want to tell me where she is?"

"I know nothing of what you're asking."

Declan rose. "We're done here."

Sacha looked smug until the guard walked in. It wasn't the one who'd brought him in.

"Finished, sir?" the guard asked.

"Yes. I believe his new arrangements have been set up?"

"Yes, sir. Solitary. No contact with the outside other than his attorney."

"Perfect." He stared at the man in the jumpsuit. "Enjoy your stay. You want to talk, have them give me a call."

Declan waited for them to shuffle off before he exited. Baldwin waited for him.

"You got to him. I'm impressed, not many can do that."

"He's a bully. Nothing more."

"He's a killer."

"Still a bully. What do you think?"

"My guess is she's in one of his homes. They have plenty of warehouses as well. I pulled a listing of his properties before I followed you here. Have it in my car."

They walked out and Declan took possession of the file. Lance crossed his arms and leaned against the side of his truck.

"I have to go over the list then."

"I'll bring dinner, you supply the beer." Baldwin smacked him on the shoulder. "Six or so. I know where you live, McBride. I'll be in touch."

"Thanks." He didn't move until the detective had pulled out. Then he tossed the file in his truck and went back inside the prison. "I need to see Angus McBride."

Before long he was in another room across from a man also in a jumpsuit. He stared at the shaved head and tattoo-covered neck and arms.

"Well, well, well. Look what we have here. If it isn't Declan McBride. Tell me, what did I do to be blessed with your presence? I mean, you never call, you never write. It's like you don't want to remember me."

The familiar Irish brogue soothed him in ways he wasn't ready to acknowledge. Maybe it was time to go home for a bit.

"What do you know about the Kazakova family?"

He sniffed and spat on the floor. "Russian scum. They all deserve to have a blade between the ribs. What do you want to know?"

"Everything."

Angus titled his head to the side. "You mixed up with them?"

"In a roundabout way. What do you know?"

His green eyes narrowed. "Trouble?"

"I wouldn't be here otherwise."

"Watch the lip, boy. You may be on that side of the table with a badge but I'm still yer elder. Show respect."

"Show some to the badge and I'll think about it."

He harrumphed, a wry grin lifting his lips. "Just like your old man. Arrogant to a fault."

"I don't have much time, Angus."

"And I have all the time in the world. What do you need, boy?"

"I need any and all information you can get on places they would hold a person. I asked Sacha but he wouldn't give me anything. I have a list of their holdings but the fucker is huge. I'm against the clock here."

"So you come to me, your uncle, the black sheep of the family for help." He leaned back. "Who is she? You wouldn't come to me if it weren't important. It's not that bitch you married, is it?"

"I'm no longer married to her and no, it isn't her."

"You bring her here to meet me and I'll tell you all I know. And will find out more. I'll send the boys out on a scouting mission."

"Deal. When I get her back, I'll bring her to meet you."

He grinned. "Always good for her to meet family."

"Clock's ticking, Angus."

"Always were impatient, boy. Fine. This is what I know."

Chapter Fourteen

She shivered and wrapped her arms around herself tighter. Caro peered through eyes that were more swollen shut than open. She was alone. Finally. Inching her way to the small toilet she then used it before hobbling back to the corner she'd been sleeping in.

The beatings were daily. Or was that hourly. She had no sense of time anymore. Didn't know if she'd been here one day or ten. All she knew was that she was scared out of her mind and wasn't sure how much longer they would keep from killing her. Or cutting off body parts.

The opening door had her stiffening instantly. She stayed as small as she could. The man who filled her line of vision was the only one who hadn't hit her. The one who wanted to keep her.

"Up."

She moved as fast as she could, not wanting him to join the ranks of her beaters. He put his fingers on the tip of her chin and angled her head, staring at the injuries.

"Clean up."

Caro didn't argue. She wanted the dried blood off her. So she padded after him. He left the room she'd been in and they stepped into a furnished area. She wanted to curl up on the couch and wrap herself in the blankets there.

He stopped by the small kitchen and handed her some paper towels. She took them, turned on the water and put them by the sink. The hot water was heaven on her skin.

She didn't rush and was grateful the man there didn't seem inclined to push her to move faster. Using the door of the microwave as a mirror, she got to work cleaning off her face.

It stung but she kept at it. While she worked, she tried not to think about how bad she looked. How much like a person who'd just been in the Octagon and got their ass kicked she appeared similar to.

She felt his presence behind her like a looming cloud. Turning to meet his gaze, she waited.

"Food here too, you cook."

A meal sounded divine. "Okay. Let me... Can I finish cleaning my face first?" *Do not piss him off. Ask instead of tell.*

"Yes."

She pivoted around and got back to it. When he put down a large towel she was surprised but didn't stop. "Thank you." There was blood on the towel after she had finished drying her face off. The cut above her eye still bled and she'd busted her lip open again during her ministrations.

He tossed the towel aside and leaned against the counter. Caro didn't even wonder much about how many weapons he had on him. She wouldn't be able to take him even if he was unarmed. The man didn't strike her as someone who let his guard down enough to be surprised.

Focused on food, she dug through the cupboards and fridge. Since he hadn't rushed her, she decided she could have something warm to eat. After she had slid the casserole in the oven, she gathered up the paper towels and opened the door below the sink to toss them out.

Her gaze lingered on the bottles of chemicals under there. Instantly she knew she could make some explosives and possibly escape. *With the amount they have down here either someone is trying to create some homemade explosives or they're just seriously germaphobic and want all the types of chemicals they can get their hands on. Then again maybe each person in a room here has a preference of what their area is cleaned with. I won't judge, I'm just glad the stuff is here.* Shutting the door, she turned away and poured herself some water. All the while her mind was streaming and doing its best to find a way to get the chemicals out and do what she had to.

Caro sat at the counter while he took a seat on the couch and turned on the television. She made herself a cup of tea and sipped it slowly.

If I make the explosion large enough the cops will arrive along with the fire department. Maybe then I can get away from these psychos. Then again maybe they're so far out from everything else, I wouldn't do anything other than piss them off for blowing up their house.

There wasn't any way to see out of the sliding glass door without being noticed. She'd have to move the curtain in order to pull it off and he looked in her direction every time she moved on the stool.

She wanted to scream in frustration. This wasn't fair. Not at all. She drank two cups before the timer went off. Her guard stood near as she set the dish on the counter. Without being asked, she got two bowls down and opened a drawer to grab some silverware. For a second, just a second she was tempted to grab a knife but she bypassed them and pulled out two forks.

His pale gaze watched her closely. *Like he expected or hoped I'd go for the knife.* Reaching back in for a spoon to serve with, she dished them both up some. He took his and dug in.

She ate slowly, still trying to work out how she was going to get the chemicals. He'd had three bowls of the casserole by the time she had finished her first one.

"Good."

She put her stuff in the sink. "Thanks."

Right at her fingertips were things she could use. Hopefully she'd get a chance to get out here to them again. It wouldn't take much for her to make them, she just needed the chance. One chance.

Someone walked in through the sliding glass door and she stared out. She could see other houses and felt another shred of hope open within her. More houses meant a better chance of cops coming with flames pouring from a house.

They talked to one another but one name caught her attention. Declan McBride. He was here. Looking for her.

"You stay here. Quiet. No one can hear you anyway." They walked out and she immediately ran to the doors, trying them. All locked.

Scrambling for the kitchen, she ignored the pain that hit her as she banged into the counter. She jerked open the doors and pulled out the cleaning supplies. She found a bucket and began pouring. The smell burned her eyes and she held her breath as she carried it to the window covering on the sliding glass door. Back in the kitchen she made another concoction. This one she put by the other door, leading to other parts of the house.

"What you do?"

The voice behind her startled her and she turned to find one man running at her. She screamed and tossed the contents of the container into his face. His cry filled the room. She couldn't figure out where he'd come from. There had to be another door. One she didn't know about.

He fumbled around for his gun and she ran toward him, jumped at him and hit him in the face. With a roar, he threw her off. She hit the corner of the island with a loud grunt. Her head bounced off the floor and she blinked away more blood as it streamed from the newly reopened cut.

She heard the whine and ducked, knowing that the explosion was imminent. Sure enough... Glass shattered and flames licked at the material around the melted container. Curtains, carpet and furniture. All went up.

A single gunshot was all she heard before she looked up to see the man, his face an ugly mess of blisters, looking in her direction. She stared down at her stomach and frowned. Her shirt wasn't red. It may have been dirty but it had been a white one.

The color spread and it hit her. *I've been shot.* She put her hand over the wound, reaching for a towel with her other to help staunch the flow, and slumped back to the floor by the island, strength escaping her with each breath she took.

She coughed and blood spewed from her lips. The man who'd shot her lay immobile. When he'd fallen she wasn't sure. More gunshots rang out and, over the roar of the growing fire, sirens pierced the air.

Her energy gone she closed her eyes. Two close shots pulled her eyes open and she looked up in time to see the other door explode as well. *What do you know, the explosive worked.*

A tall figure ducked through the hole that had been made, even as she stared at the splinters scattered around her.

"Caro?"

She didn't have the energy to speak. Her blood, warm and sticky, flowed between her fingers to coat more of her shirt and skin. Turning her tired eyes up it took a few seconds for recognition to sink in.

Declan. He was there, approaching her. Bulletproof vest strapped on, amplifying the strength in his upper body, his white shirt below it a stark contrast to the black material keeping him safe.

"Oh shit!" He sank beside her, concern all over his face. "Hang on, Caro. Hang on."

I wish you didn't hate me, Declan. I wish I had the strength to tell you all the things I didn't have the guts to tell you before. She couldn't find her words. There was no hope for her to locate and share them with the man before her. Black spots flecked the corners of her eyes.

"This is going to hurt, baby, but I have to get you out of here before the fire gets any closer."

He lifted her up in his arms. With the remaining bits of her energy she took her hand and touched the side of his face. *Thank you, Declan McBride. Thank you for not letting me die here.* Her hand fell back to her belly as he maneuvered them past the door and fairly sprinted up the stairs. The sunlight hit her skin as he moved them through the chaos surrounding them.

She closed her eyes as he shouted for a medic.

* * * *

Declan was a man who'd seen a lot of death and disturbing situations given his job. He wasn't squeamish and he wasn't timid. He'd always soldiered through everything thrown at him. However, this — *this* was totally different.

He had never been so scared in his life.

"Put her here!" an EMT yelled at him.

Blinking, Declan placed her down on the stretcher. Immediately the men shoved him to the side and worked on her.

"We have to get moving with her or we're going to lose her."

"Make sure you don't," he growled low, grabbing one man by the arm.

"Are you injured?"

"I'm fine. It's not my blood, it's hers." All hers. And there was so much of it.

"We're going." They didn't wait for him to say anything and as much as he wanted to go with her, Baldwin was still in there and he wasn't going to leave him behind.

Declan whirled around and with hands on his lightweight automatic he ran back inside the house.

"Where are you, Baldwin?"

He made his way up the marble staircase, waiting for his answer via the ear piece.

"Third floor. Hurry."

Behind him more uniformed officers burst through the door. He didn't wait for them, instead took the stairs, several at a time. The smoke from outside had begun to filter in to where he was. "Location?"

"Left at the top, third door on the right."

He made his way there. "Coming in."

Declan pushed the door open slowly and crept in. Baldwin stood across the room, black shoes on the gold carpet. Their gazes met and Declan raised his eyebrow in silent question. Baldwin held up his hand, fingers spread before indicating the door — the only other one in the room.

At least five people. Armed.

He grinned when Lance exchanged his pistol for the shotgun that had been on his back. They changed positions and with his hand signal countdown they breached the room.

Baldwin took out the hinges with two spot-on hits from the shotgun he wielded. Declan had his DDM4 V5 up and trained on the stunned occupants.

"Weapons down! Weapons down!" he yelled.

"On the ground! On the ground!" Baldwin's voice echoed his.

It didn't take the group long to get over the shock of the door being blown off its hinges, and the bullets started flying.

Shit! Lunging to the right he shot in short bursts, ensuring not to put any into Lance. There may have been five at the start but from another door more came in, shooting. They fell back to some cover using the wall on either side of the door Declan and the detective had entered from, continuing to exchange fire.

Footsteps thundered up the stairs behind them. Declan turned in time to see a young female officer burst in. His world succumbed into slow motion as he lunged for her.

One man lifted his MP5 and fired. Declan hit the woman as the first slug entered his hip. Two more buried in him as he bore her to the ground. Biting back his grunt of pain he covered her as best he could as more cops entered the room and turned the tide of the gun battle.

The gunfire ceased and Baldwin's face came into view.

"Hang in there. Bus is coming."

"Caro." Declan's words were slurred.

"I'll find out on the way to get you there." He settled his hand on his shoulder. "Stay with me."

"What do we got?" A black woman came into his view.

"Multiple gunshots."

She nodded. "I see that. Least you wore your vest. Tell me your name."

"Declan. McBride."

"Nice to meet you, Declan McBride. Are you allergic to anything?"

They rolled him onto the stretcher and got him moving. "Lead."

She smiled at him as they collapsed the trolley for the stairs. "Aren't we all. Glad to see you've maintained your sense of humor. That's wonderful."

"Caro?" He tried to ask around the oxygen they gave him.

Baldwin's voice faded in and out. Declan couldn't make out his words as the darkness finally managed to blanket him.

* * * *

He went from asleep to awake in an instant. Casting his gaze around the room, Declan saw LT in a chair mixing what had to be coffee—the man lived off the stuff—with a wooden stirrer.

"Wouldn't have to stir it so much if you didn't dump half a canister of sugar in each cup you drank."

LT smiled as he looked over at him. "'Bout time you woke up, you lazy bastard." LT moved near. "How are you feeling?"

"Like I got shot multiple times."

"You did. So your memory's fine."

Declan touched the tubes running out of his nose and glared at his lieutenant.

"Hang tight. I'll get a nurse in here."

Within the hour, Declan was sitting up a bit more in the hospital bed listening to LT wrap up the rest of his explanation of what had gone down.

He cleared his throat, which turned into a coughing fit. Two nurses stood over him by the time he had finished. He raised his eyebrow and stared at them both. "I'm fine."

Neither took his word for it and checked him over. Once they had left, he settled back against the mattress. Lance walked in carrying a bag of fast food.

"Sup?" He raked him from head to toe. "You look like shit."

"I'm in a hospital bed, what's your excuse?"

LT chuckled while Baldwin tsked and held up the bag. "Be nice or I keep the fries and shake I smuggled in here."

"You didn't smuggle shit in here. You just walked by the nurses out there, flirted a bit and kept going," Declan said.

The man didn't look the least bit perturbed by his assessment. In fact he grinned wide. "Use what you have to your advantage. You wouldn't know about that, being an ugly Irishman."

Declan beckoned for the bag. "Hand it over, jackass." Working together had moved them into a realm where he'd actually consider them to be friends.

They set it up on the table and he groaned in pleasure as he ate his first bite. "How's Caro?"

There wasn't any way for him to miss the exchanged look between the two men. He placed his cheeseburger down and flicked his glance between the both of them.

"What the fuck aren't you telling me?"

"She's okay, Declan. She'll live." Lance touched his arm gently.

He had to relax and it took several deep breaths before he could find his way to do that. "So what's with the looks?"

"She's not here, so don't ask to see her."

"What do you mean she's not here? Where the fuck is she?" He struggled to get up, shoving the wheeled table out of his way.

Both LT and Baldwin halted his weak attempt to get off the bed. "Stay put, McBride. You're in no condition to walk."

"So get me a fucking wheelchair. I want to see her."

His lieutenant shook his head. "Like Detective Baldwin said, she's not here."

"Where. Is. She?"

"She went home."

"She was able to check out of the hospital?"

"Not exactly. As soon as she was stable enough to be moved she was transferred."

His eyes grew wide. "A transfer is from local hospital to local hospital. Not halfway across the country."

"She went back to Wisconsin. She's in the hospital at the university. It's where she wanted to go and where her parents wanted her to go."

Pain exploded in his hip and he winced. "I need to go up there and see for myself."

They exchanged another look and Baldwin took a seat while LT heaved a sigh. "You can't."

"Why not?"

"You can't walk for a while. In fact, you will be in rehab for a long time." LT shoved a hand through his hair. "Depending on how it goes, you may be on a desk for the rest of your career."

Ice settled around his heart. A desk? He hadn't joined the blue brotherhood to ride a desk. Just like he'd never wanted to become a detective because he loved where he was. He wanted to do what he did. Not something else.

"I'm sorry, son."

So was he. "I need to think about this."

LT nodded and walked away, pausing once to look at Baldwin who didn't move from his seat. Then he vanished from view.

"Something you need, Baldwin?"

"Yep. This is for you." He stood and reached in his pocket. Handing over the paper he'd withdrawn he gave a sharp nod of his head. "Call if you need me. Thanks for having my back out there."

The man left him alone. "No, man. Thank you."

Exhausted by the news and his condition, Declan shut his eyes, the paper in his hand, scrunching. He took several deep breaths and opened the folded sheet. Caro's handwriting jumped off the paper at him.

Chapter Fifteen

"Are you sure you're all right, sweetheart?"

Caro looked at the man who'd raised her from a baby. A proud man. A loving man. Her father. "I'm fine, Daddy." *Maybe if I say it enough times I'll believe it.* "How are you and Mama?"

He held her hand, his strength familiar and comforting. "Don't worry about us, we need you to get better."

"I'm sorry." She wiped at the stinging tears. "I'm so sorry I didn't tell you about Jasmine."

"Don't worry about that, sweetheart. You had your reasons. We're just so thrilled you're okay."

Was she? The jury was still out on that debate. But if it kept more concern and worry from her parents she would continue to lie about it until she could no longer do so. With the smile still pasted in place, she squeezed his hand.

"Aren't you supposed to be at work, Daddy?"

"You know, my boss actually gave me some time to spend with my daughter."

"Nice man, your boss," she said, her smile becoming more real instead of forced. Her father worked for himself.

"I think so."

She readjusted so her head rested upon his arm and took a deep breath, ignoring the lance of pain from her stomach area. "I just wanted to help her."

His lips brushed her forehead. "Of course you did, Carolyn. That's how we raised you. To help others. Why wouldn't you help your twin?"

"I also feel angry, Daddy. So very angry."

"Terri says that's natural."

"I know she does. Doesn't mean I feel right having those feelings."

"You, sweetheart, have a heart of gold. It doesn't matter you spend most of your days hidden away in a lab concocting something or another. Your heart is pure. And you should have no guilt for what happened. None." He smoothed some of her hair back. "We checked the papers and they rounded up a lot of his crew. That guy isn't getting out. In fact there was some skirmish at the prison where a big group of his men were taken down by the Irish faction in there."

She opened her eyes and stared at her father. "Irish?"

He nodded, his brown eyes somber. "According to reports, it was some kind of gang war inside the walls."

Declan.

"I see." Her words were barely above a whisper.

"Get some rest. I'll be right here." Another brushed kiss on her head.

"Love you, Daddy."

"Love you too, sweetheart."

She lay as close as she could to his arm and closed her eyes, his scent comforting her as it had when she was younger, spiriting her away to the land of sleep and Hypnos.

* * * *

Terri sat beside her when she woke next.

"Hey."

"What are you doing here?" Caro asked.

"Came to visit and bring flowers." She gestured over her shoulder.

Tracking her movement, Caro discovered a large vase of vibrant-hued flowers. She smiled as she took in the mixture of roses, lilies, sunflowers and more. "Beautiful, thank you."

"Not from me, I just brought them up. From my office."

"Your people are so good to me."

Terri laughed. "They love you there. You always bring them sweets when you come. And we all feel horrible about what happened."

"You deserve the credit, Terri. You called him. I'm just glad they didn't smash into your place as well."

"You know I'm here if you need to talk."

"I know. And I appreciate it. But I think this is something I have to work through on my own."

"I'll save the professional speech and just say okay." She paused. "This time. But if I think you need it and you're not coming. I'm coming to you. I won't lose my best friend."

"I'm not going anywhere."

"Better not. We have plans to fulfill yet."

"I know."

"Did your dad tell you about what he read in the paper?"

She readjusted her bed. "Yes. Have you heard anything else?"

"Not a peep. I could call back down there and enquire if you'd like me too."

"No. I don't think that would be a good idea."

"Okay. I won't push that."

"Thanks."

"Now, are you ready to leave? You can go home today. That's why I'm here. I'm taking you. Your parents wanted to set something special up for you."

"I'd figured."

They checked her out and she moved slowly from the wheelchair to the front seat of Terri's BMW SUV. Buckling her seatbelt, she stared at the falling snow. Terri hopped in and got them moving. Part of her wanted to cry but more of her wanted to move on. She'd said her goodbyes to Declan and her thank you for what he'd done. He had come for her.

* * * *

Caro sat at the window of her apartment. Her landlord had offered for her to move into a different one, even in another of his buildings, based on what had happened. She'd refused — part of the reason she'd taken this one to begin with was because of her view. She loved it.

Her bags were beside her and she waited for Terri to come to the door. She had a trip to take. All those long nights of lying awake and thinking about Declan had eaten at her. She had to see if she could wrangle up a face to face with him.

"Ready?"

Bending, she grabbed the handles of her duffle and said, "As I'll ever be. Thanks for driving me."

"No problem. Can I assume you're only taking one bag because you don't plan on being clothed most of the time?"

Caro laughed and rolled her eyes. "You have sex on the brain, Doc. You should see your boyfriend about that."

"He's in Vladivostok for another week before he comes home." A wink. "If you come back and your battery supply is depleted, I'll owe you some."

"Yes you will."

Together they headed down, and in Terri's vehicle kept up the light-hearted banter. Caro hopped out at the airport and waved to her friend as she walked inside. At her gate, she pulled out her Kindle and started reading a book, one that would normally keep her attention for she was a huge fan of the author, but this time, her concentration was nil.

Her flights were uneventful and as she slipped behind the wheel of her rental she was nervous. What if he wasn't there? What if he slammed the door in her face?

"Oh suck it up, Caro. Get out there and find out for yourself."

She got on the road and drove carefully, grateful they were at least plowed. They weren't in the best of condition but it was better than she'd been expecting, honestly. Darkness had fallen when she pulled into the small town. She parked before the first place she'd visited when she had been here before and shut off the engine. The town was still as silent as it had been then.

"Stop procrastinating. Get going."

She took the keys and climbed out. Walking up to the door, she gazed around. Not a person in sight.

With a deep breath, she opened the door and stepped inside the warm building.

"Be right with you."

She waited near the entrance for Martin to appear.

"What can I help you with tod—" He slowed to a stop. "Caro." He looked beyond her. "What are you doing here?"

"I need to find Declan. Is he here?"

Martin approached and guided her to his desk where he pushed her into a chair. Seconds later she had a steaming cup of coffee before her as Martin sat on his desk.

"You're looking for Declan?"

"Yes. Is he at his cabin, Martin?"

"No. At least not that I know of. He's not been in contact with me if he did come back. I just saw Tasha and she didn't say he was home either."

"How is she doing?"

"Learning to be a single mom. But okay. I'll tell her you enquired after her."

The words weren't spoken aloud but she knew he didn't feel right about her being there. She drank her coffee before she spoke again. "I know my being here is a problem for you, Martin, and I'm sorry. I just…needed to thank him in person as opposed to the note I used before. That's all." She stood. "I'm sorry to have bothered you."

Heart breaking, she walked to the door and slipped through without a glance back. She was tired but it didn't matter, she had to return to the airport. As she started the engine, she decided to swing by his place just to see for herself. If there was no sign of life, she would head back. If there was, she'd suck up her fear and go knock on his door.

* * * *

"Got a minute?"

Declan rolled his eyes at the feminine voice. "What do you want, Jackie?" He continued to put items in his box.

"Why are you quitting the force? You're a hero." She appeared in his line of sight.

"None of your business why I do anything." He stared at the picture of him and some of his fellow brothers. With a puff he added it to the box.

"You know we were good together." She lifted out one of his first commendations. "I remember when you got this."

He snatched it back. "What do you want? Is this a now I'm finally worthy of the great and powerful Jacquelyn Ashcraft because I'm known as a hero for what I did? Because if that's what you're here for you can turn your bottle blonde ass around and leave. I'm not interested. I've been on that ride and it wasn't a fun one."

Her green gaze hardened. "No need to be an ass."

"Why not? You've been a bitch the entire time. Why are you allowed but I'm not."

"You know I'm an ADA."

"Oohhh. Ladeefuckingdah. Congratulations. I'm a man who doesn't give a fuck. Are you here for a real reason or just looking out for number one again?"

She ground her jaw and normally he would back off but right now, he didn't care in the slightest that she was angry. So was he.

"I wanted to say there's a PI spot available for the DA's office if you're interested."

He lifted one eyebrow and held her gaze. "Put myself in a position where you can give me orders?

Thanks but no thanks." He dropped in the last of his stuff and stepped closer to her, voice dropping. "You're all about you, Jackie, and that's fine. You do you. But I'm not giving you that kind of say over me. Thanks for thinking of me, if that's even why it came up—which I highly doubt—but I'm going to have to decline the generous offer." He leaned closer. "I can't live like you, not giving a damn who gets hurt along the way as long as your record doesn't suffer. Have a good life, ADA Ashcraft."

Declan picked up his box and walked to the door. The men and women in the area watched him, his old LT included. He didn't slow, didn't stop to look at them. He'd already said his goodbyes, no need to do so again.

He took the elevator down, his hip hurting him, and rested the box on the bar as the car moved. Limping to his truck, he wondered how he would make the adjustment. He'd been a cop for so long he didn't know how to be anything else.

"Something to think about later," he muttered.

He drove away from precinct for the last time and didn't even bother trying to justify the pricks of tears in his eyes. He'd loved his job, there'd been no doubt about that. At his home, he set the box in his office then walked out of the room, shutting the door decisively behind him.

Slumped on the couch, he dangled a beer in his hand as he stared at the television. His phone rang and he ignored it, draining the rest of his drink. Three more times it rang. On the fourth time, he reached for the handset and snarled into it.

"What do you want?"

"Is that any way to answer a phone?"

Martin. "What do you want, Martin?"

"Just wanted to let you know your woman came here."

"My woman?"

"Caro."

He sat upright in a flash. "Caro? Came there?"

"She said she was looking for you. I told her you weren't here."

"Is she still there?"

"Nope. She left. Swung by your cabin, though. Guess she didn't believe me when I said you weren't around."

"How'd she look?"

An understanding chuckle left his friend. "Sad. Definitely not as full of fire as she was previously. What happened to her?"

"A lot, Martin. A lot. She was shot a few times and almost died." Christ, it still made him sick to his stomach to think about that day. His final in a uniform.

"You should find her, son. Find her and get her back. You both sound like shit."

"Why would she want me? I'm jobless and I told her I never wanted to see her again."

"Who saved her?"

"I carried her to the ambulance."

"And you found her why? Because you were looking for her."

That was true. They had been doing a property by property search for her. If that explosion hadn't happened when it had he would have left never knowing she was being held prisoner there."

"She's a fighter, she would have been found."

"So you tell her all you did and still save her? Seems to me, son, if you'd get your head out of your ass you would see what I do."

"Which is?"

"She loves you. Why else would she come all the way out here looking for you? Lord, you young people sure are stupid at times."

"You really think she loves me?"

"Declan, it don't matter what I think. It all matters what you think and the actions you take because of that belief. Me, though... If I had a woman who would track me down out here just to say thank you face to face, I'm thinking there's a bit more there to it than just gratitude."

"Thanks, Martin."

"Go get her, kid."

The call ended and Declan smiled as he hung up the receiver. "I plan on it."

He went to his closet and changed into some clean clothes. The knock on his door gave him pause as he shoved his cell phone and wallet into his pants. Opening it, he groaned with disbelief.

"Wasn't once a day enough, Jackie?"

"We need to talk about this, McBride."

"You have your car?"

"Not mine but the job's car service, so yes. Why?"

"Good, I have somewhere to be, we can talk on the way."

"Okay." They rode down the elevator in silence and at the car, he slid in first.

"Where to?" she asked.

"Airport."

"You heard him, Karl. Drive to the airport."

"Yes, ma'am."

Jackie looked at him and crossed her legs. "Why are you so determined to ignore our past?"

"Ignore it? I'm not. What I'm doing is called moving on. Remember? You told me to do that when you left my bed for that other man's."

She flushed. "So I wasn't the best wife in the world. But we were good together."

He shook his head. "Let me stop you before you even go further. I'm not helping you boost your career. I'm not the man for that, Jackie. Let it go. You don't get to shove people to the side then expect them to come crawling back and be grateful to do so just because you put some attention their way. We're finished. There's no second chance anything."

"You don't have to be so crass."

He laughed. "That's not crass. Trust me, I've cleaned it up a lot out of respect for your driver. You know me, Jackie. I don't give a damn about a lot of things. I cared about you and my badge. You killed that when you cheated on our vows. You cheated because I wouldn't seek out the title you wanted me to have. If you thought sleeping with a detective would get me motivated to get the shield you were sorely mistaken. I loved you. Loved. Past tense. Don't anymore and I'm not willing to be pawn to your social and political climbing."

"Nothing I say will ever change that fact, will it?"

"Here's fine," he told the driver who pulled up to the airport. He opened the door and glanced over at his ex-wife. "Nope. Never. Have a good life, Jackie. Thanks for the lift."

"Wait," she said.

He stuck his head back in. "Yes?"

"No luggage. What are you doing at the airport?"

"Catching a flight. There's a woman I need to see about a happily ever after." He slammed the door and jogged to the entrance of the airport. At the counter he said, "I need the first flight to Madison, Wisconsin, please. Your line and the others."

Chapter Sixteen

Caro sat before her computer typing on the keyboard, entering her latest findings. She rolled her shoulders, trying to alleviate the tension and stiffness.

"You should go home."

"Thanks, Thad. I will as soon as I finish entering this information." She glanced over at him. "What are you still doing here?"

"Same as you. Entering data."

They shared wry smiles. Thad Claire was a great co-worker. He wasn't one who wanted to prove himself as smarter than the women. He wanted to do his job. Well. The man was super-intelligent and she genuinely liked him as a person.

She stood and stretched. "Well, I need coffee, can I bring you anything?"

"Coffee would be awesome. And some kind of candy bar. I need some energy or I'm going to fall asleep right here."

"Got it. Be right back."

She walked slowly down the hall and when her phone rang, she didn't stop, just answered it. "Hey, girl." Terri had her own ring.

"Hey. When are you getting home?"

She entered their break room. "No clue. Probably not for about two hours or so. I'm in the middle of entering my data. Well, not right now, right now I'm getting coffee and candy for myself and Thad. Why?"

"I left something for you in your place and I have some food I'm going to heat up for you. Call me when you're about to leave and I'll take it over and put it in the oven."

"You're the best."

"I know."

Caro laughed. "And so modest. What'd you leave for me?"

"Something I think you'll like. I know you will. I'm taking batteries as payment."

She poured their coffee. "I should be worried you know where my batteries are."

"I should be worried you have such a large collection of them."

She snorted. "You should be thankful. I'm apparently buying them for two."

"You're the one with the extensive collection, I just have—"

"Lalalalala, I don't want to know." Caro smiled as she fixed Thad's drink and grabbed him two candy bars. A Snickers and a Whatchamacallit.

"Come back soon and don't forget, call me when you're ready to leave there."

"Will do and thanks again, hon."

"No problem."

She hung up and walked back to the room. Thad thanked her and they got back to work.

As promised she called Terri as she finished up and got ready to leave. She and Thad walked outside in the snowy night.

"See you later, Carolyn."

"Night, Thad." She climbed into her vehicle and sent up thanks she had automatic start for it was warm and she got on her way. At her apartment building, she parked in her spot and made her way up to her door. Fighting a yawn, she unlocked it and let herself in.

The air smelled of manicotti and garlic bread. Her stomach growled in anticipation. *Bless you, Terri.* Setting her keys in the bowl beside the door, she toed off her shoes and flipped on a light.

"Wonder where she put this package she said was waiting for me?"

"Right here."

She screamed before she realized who stood in her place. Declan McBride. Hungrily she trailed her gaze over him as he stepped from the shadows into the light. Scruff on his jaw made him appear darker even. His harsh features seemed gaunter than when she had seen him last. Still, he had those same broad shoulders and lean hips. Past him she saw his black leather jacket hanging over the back of her sofa.

She ogled his jeans—looser than usual, yet still not doing anything to hide the powerful legs. His dark blue Henley had its sleeves pushed up showing off the dark hair on his muscled forearms.

"Declan."

"Caro."

Torn between her desire to run into his arms or hook her own around her waist to keep from touching him and letting him see how much she trembled, she stayed where she was. "Wha... What are you doing here?"

"Looking for you."

"You didn't want to see me again."

He walked toward her with a limp on his right side. He obviously knew she had noticed it when he pulled up. "Does it bother you? My limp?"

"What happened?"

"Shot. Pins."

Her gaze widened. "Because of me?" *I ruined his career.*

"No. A young officer ran into the line of fire. I pushed her out of the way."

"But at the house I set on fire."

His stare remained fixated on her face. "Yes. I'm so glad you did."

"You were shot."

His gaze darkened. "So were you. I watched you bleeding out." He stepped closer and nearly reached out to touch her but dropped his hand back to his side.

"You saved me. I remembered seeing you there."

A tortured expression filled his features. "I almost drove away. Had you not set the fire..." He shook his head. "I don't want to think about what would have happened to you."

"My being shot wasn't your fault, Declan. I told you that in the note. And I said thank you because I knew it was you who rescued me. You have nothing to feel guilty over."

Another step. "That's where you're wrong, Carolyn Trufant. There's so much I have to make amends for."

She swallowed. "Is that why you're here? To clear your conscience?"

"Is that why you tried to find me in the mountains?"

Caro shook her head. "You don't get to counter my question with one of your own."

Was it her imagination or did she see sparks of amusement in his blue-green eyes?

"I don't?"

"No."

He put them toe to toe and she had to tip her head back to maintain visual contact. Her body trembled as she filled her nose with his masculine scent. It had been so long since she'd smelled it. She wanted to rub in it until it seeped into her pores and she carried his scent with her. On her. Around her.

"Very well. No, that's not why I came."

"Why did you come?"

"Don't I get a question now?"

Her fingers burned to touch him. *If he's restraining, I can as well. I'm not a whore. Right? Right. I can control my needs.* "Fine, ask it."

"Why did you come looking for me in the mountains?"

"I wanted to thank you in person. The note I'd sent seemed a bit impersonal given all you'd done for me."

Flames licked his eyes. "Was that the only reason?"

"I answered you, now you answer me. Why did you come?" Lord help her she wasn't sure she could tell him the other reason she'd gone after him.

"I needed to see for myself that you were okay. I needed to make sure and I needed to talk to you." He closed his eyes briefly as if he was pausing to find some strength from somewhere. "I needed to tell you something important."

It lingered on the tip of her tongue to ask what it was. She stared at his bow-shaped lips and dug her toes into her socks. What she wouldn't give to feel them on her once more.

"Now, was that the only reason?"

"No." She dragged her tongue along her lower lip. His eyes tracked the motion and she posed her question. "Will you kiss me?"

His mouth had settled over hers before the words had even faded from the air. She sighed into him and leaned in, trusting he would hold her up. Declan slid his hands along the sides of her face before sinking them into her hair and holding her close. She whimpered as his taste flooded her again, at long last. Digging her fingers into his upper arms she pressed herself as near to him as she could manage.

"Caro," he whispered along her lips.

She opened her eyes to find him staring at her. "I know, I'm not what you want. I lied to you."

She stepped back only to find it wasn't possible. He wouldn't let her get away.

"Don't put words in my mouth."

"You're the one who said them. I was merely restating."

"I was an idiot and an ass. There's no other woman I want than you, Caro. You. Not your twin. You. I fell in love with you during that time out at the cabin. At first I thought you were just trying to play and get me to drop my guard so you could run off again. The more I watched you — and I did a lot of that — the more I realized the goodness you had. At the time, it didn't make sense how you could have been so different than the person I remember Jasmine being. It does now. You're not her."

"How can you be in love with me? You didn't even know it was me."

The corners of his mouth turned up. "The thing is, I fell for the woman you were. And again, that was you. Not Jasmine. I saw your eyes light up at things I never thought you would like. Snow. Seclusion. Playing games in front of the fire." He touched their foreheads. "Making cranes."

"Wasn't too fond of the spider."

She received a full grin from him for that. His white teeth flashed against his tanned skin.

"I'm grateful for the view you gave me."

She ducked her head and put it against his chest. Closing her eyes, she breathed deeply when he wrapped his arms around her. Contentment and peace flowed through her.

Declan didn't want to move from this spot but his hip was screaming at him. He ignored it as best he could. Hell, she was back in his arms, he could withstand anything. He didn't ignore the fact she'd not said she loved him back.

"I have to get the food out." Her words were muffled from going into his shirt.

"Okay." He let her go and followed her into her kitchen. While he'd been waiting for her to return, he'd taken himself on a tour of her place. Her cranes were everywhere. All colors and all types of paper.

Her bookcase was full of chemistry books and things that made his eyes cross to attempt to read. He saw her degrees framed on her bedroom wall and realized she'd not lied to him that day. In fact she hadn't lied to him once. She had told him she wasn't Jasmine—he was the one who had opted not to believe her.

Now that he knew the difference it was more of a shock to him that he hadn't picked up on the fact they were two separate people. Jasmine was a bottle of pent-up energy. Caro was calmness personified.

He'd stared at the pictures of the people who had adopted and raised her. The love in that family was so blatant even through the image. She had pictures of Terri up as well. And a man Terri had told him was her boyfriend. They were a close-knit group. He understood that now and also got how hard it must have been for Caro to do what she had done for Jasmine.

There weren't a lot of knick-knacks around her place and he got the feeling that was intentional. Other than the cranes, of course. She was an amazing woman.

"Did you eat or are you joining me?"

"Joining."

"Grab a seat."

Over the meal he kept the talk to questions about what she did. He wanted to be able to hold her when he discussed their future. Declan assisted with the clean-up then after she had shut the door to the dishwasher, he grabbed her hand and took her to the couch. Before them, the fire burned strong, and to his left snow fell outside the window.

He gathered her close and pressed his lips to her temple. "I love you, Carolyn Trufant. I don't want to live without you any longer."

She maneuvered so that she straddled him and rested her arms on his shoulders, fingers teasing the nape of his neck. His cock became rigid as he grunted slightly when she shifted over it.

"What does that mean? You want me to move to Atlanta?"

"We could live there if you wanted. Madison seems like a nice city. You're settled here, family and friends."

"You are in Atlanta."

"Nope. I'm not a cop anymore. I didn't want to ride a desk and with this limp and pins in my hip I can't be on the streets anymore."

"I'm sorry."

He shook his head. "No. This isn't your fault." A dry chuckle left him. "Look at us. Both shot multiple times. Both recovering and learning to live again. I want to learn it with you. I'll find something else to do, Caro. All I know right now is it's you I need in my life."

"You don't see Jasmine when you look at me?"

"Not a chance. I barely saw Jasmine when I saw her. I had no use for her. You, Caro, I see. Do you understand what I'm saying? I see you."

She closed her eyes and he didn't know what to do with the tears that leaked over the corners. Caro touched his lips. "I love you too, Declan."

Those five words freed the rest of his heart and soul. The remaining weight on him lifted away.

He slid his hands up under her blouse. She moaned against his lips. "I need a shower. Care to join me?"

"I don't have any other clothes with me."

"You should probably take these off then." She climbed off his lap and unbuttoned her top. He became mesmerized by the dark skin she exposed, her breasts covered by the lacy bra. With a roll of her shoulders the silk pooled at her feet.

He rumbled low in his chest. She stepped farther back and beckoned with her fingers, even as she unfastened her pants. He lurched off the sofa and followed her down the hall to her bathroom. As she walked through the door, her slacks hit the floor and she walked on, her white—also lacy—boy shorts barely covering the globes of her ass.

Declan ripped off his Henley and dropped it. He made short work of untying his boots and taking them off. Fingers on the button of his jeans he paused as her bra sailed back to hit his bare toes. He stared at her, bending over slightly to adjust the water in her shower stall. Her ass tempted him so much and when she stood upright, he watched as she hooked her thumbs in the material and slowly lowered it to the ground before stepping free.

She peered over her shoulder at him, smiled then entered the shower. He watched her through the glass as she stood under the water.

"Coming?"

Just about. He finally removed his pants and boxers. Touching his scars, he hoped they wouldn't bother her and went to join her in the shower. She stood there, facing him, head tipped back as she wetted her hair. His cock jerked as he roved over her body with his gaze.

He lingered on her own scars then focused back on her face in time to see her open her eyes. The siren's smile curving up her lips stiffened his shaft even more.

"Just going to look or do you plan on touching?" She dragged her fingers over her breasts and down to her pussy.

"Touching," he rasped. "Definitely touching."

"Get to it then."

He did. He closed the distance between them and kissed her as he palmed her breasts. She moaned as he manipulated the tips between his fingers, tugging, rolling and pinching.

Her hands dug into his shoulders as she moved beneath his touch. She nipped at his tongue and he drew back. "I don't have any condoms."

"Me either." She fisted his cock and worked her hand up and down. "Not a single one in this place. I could go ask Terri for some."

He took one nipple in his mouth, drawing hard on it. Her cry was music to his ears.

"I don't think we need to bring her into this," he said around her tip. A light nip and he released her.

"Although I am curious to know about all those toys in your drawer."

"Get me out of here and we can go see."

He reached around her and shut off the water. Declan lifted her into his arms and she wrapped her legs about his waist. Her slickness rubbed against him with each step he took. In her room, he dropped her on the bed and was over her instantly. She guided him to her.

"Protection?" he croaked.

"Please," she begged, eyes dark with need and desire. "Declan, I need you."

He surged forward with one thrust and filled her. His groan was matched by one from her. She was so snug around him. So perfect.

Reclaiming one of her breasts, he thrust his hips. In and out. She writhed beneath him, undulating in time to his movements.

He fitted her. She was made for him. Back and forth he moved, withdrawing until just the head of his cock sat in her then filling her as full as he could with his next drive forwards.

Her cries, a euphonious sound, neared a crescendo and her internal walls rippled around his turgid length. She dug her nails into his shoulders, back bowing, and screamed his name to her room as she came around him. Forcefully.

His balls had drawn tight and he drove deep one more time as his seed burst free. She trembled again and her moisture coated him as she rode out yet another climax.

He sagged onto her, covering her with his larger body. His heart pounded. He kissed her neck before moving onto her lips. Full, lush, his. He couldn't imagine not having this woman in his life. Not anymore. She was his. He was hers.

Taking his time, he enjoyed and explored her mouth. Saying without words that which his heart needed to convey to her. And not just his heart but also his soul. Both of which belonged to her. He licked the sides and roof, danced with her tongue and touched all he could reach.

Her purr rumbled up from deep in her chest to his mouth. His cock began to harden inside her pussy once more.

"Love you," she whispered as she braced her feet on the mattress.

"Love you, too." Declan moved, ready to begin this journey with her all over again. He couldn't get enough of her.

And I never will.

Chapter Seventeen

Caro sighed and took another lick of her chocolate ice cream. The day was perfect, the blue sky nearly cloudless aside from a few fluffy ones that lingered here and there. A gentle breeze blew off the lake and offered some respite to those gathered.

Tonight was the large Fourth of July celebration. She checked her watch again and shrugged. *Wonder what's keeping him.*

"Waiting for someone?" A decadent male voice wound around her with the question.

She smiled and took another leisurely lick of her ice cream. "I am."

"Who would that be?"

"My boyfriend. He's late, though."

"Foolish man. I hope he makes it up to you." Lips teased her neck and she closed her eyes in bliss.

"I'm sure he will."

"As am I." He nipped her skin before planting another kiss there.

When she opened her eyes she found herself staring at a large bouquet of red roses, white daisy poms and blue delphiniums. All surrounded by a yellow ribbon and a bear with a red, white and blue scarf around its neck.

She turned to face Declan. His blue-green eyes sparkled in the sun and she leaned forward to kiss him on the lips. "Thank you for the flowers, they're beautiful. What's the occasion?"

"None other than it's the Fourth. I saw these and thought you could use some."

She took them from him and dipped her head to partake in the fragrance wafting from them. He used the tip of his finger to bring her gaze back up to his.

"Are you okay?"

She drew him down to the seat next to her and willingly handed over her ice cream when he reached for it. For a few moments she lost herself in watching his sure tongue swipes as he indulged in the treat.

"Caro?"

She smiled and blushed. "I'm fine. Just got a lot on my mind right now. How are you?"

"Nice try, baby, you don't get to get a pass that easily. Something's bothering you. What is it? Can I help?"

"Jasmine called."

His expression sobered. "I thought she was in witness protection and not supposed to have contact with any of those from her past."

"She is and she's not, yet she did."

He shook his head. "Of course she did. Woman doesn't know how to follow the rules." They stared out over the lake. "How is she doing?"

"She wanted to make sure we were doing fine."

"That's nice of her."

"Yeah. I don't know, Declan. I honestly expect her to show up one day."

"Your sister is a force all to her own. She may someday. Do you not want to see her again?"

"No, that's not it at all. It's just hard. I mean, I didn't have her for nearly thirty-four years, found her then lost her again. I'm not sure how to feel."

"Look, I know she isn't the easiest woman to deal with. But despite all her crazy psycho ideas, she loves you. You are the one thing which will have the capabilities of encouraging her to become a decent person in society."

She rested her head on his shoulder. "You always know just what to say."

"Not hardly but I can see things clearly from the outside." He brushed a kiss on her forehead. "Don't worry. All will work out."

"So what's bothering you?"

"Meaning?"

"I heard you this morning arguing with someone on the phone about bringing me to visit."

He stiffened and she tipped her head back to watch him.

"Members of my family want to meet you."

"You don't want to introduce me to them?"

"Not particularly, no."

"Oh." She'd not been expecting such pain to pierce her at his response.

"No, you don't understand, Caro. This part of my family is in prison."

"And I would judge because my twin is a drug addict and from all accounts a whore?"

"This is more than drugs and prostitution."

She tugged him down so she could reach his ear. Dragging her tongue along the edge of it she smiled softly. "I know. They're the ones who took care of things in the prison so you could come find me. I want to meet them."

He met her gaze. "You knew?"

"Had a hunch when I heard what happened in the prison. My daddy mentioned it and I looked deeper into it."

"You don't mind I have ties to organized crime?"

"You, Declan McBride, are you. I love you. It's that simple. You were an honorable cop for over twenty years. That's all I need to know."

"You're a pretty amazing woman, Carolyn Trufant."

"I know. But I've got one hell of a man who helps that be reality."

His gaze darkened. "How much time do we have before the fireworks start?"

"More than enough."

He stood abruptly and pulled her along with him. She allowed him to set the pace back to their apartment and once they'd arrived there. His hunger had an edge to it today and she reveled in it, taking all she could and asking for more. Bless the man, for he never hesitated, just gave her all she could take and then some.

After they'd showered and changed into different clothing she stood by the large window and stared out over her city. This place sang to her in ways nowhere else did. She loved it here. Thrived here.

"You look very pensive again. Are you sure everything's okay?"

She glanced over to the man who meant the world to her. "I'm fine. Do you ever miss your cabin?"

His expression told of his confusion. "You want me to go to the cabin?"

"I'm wondering if you miss it. Would you like to go there for a while?"

"You'd go with me?"

"Unless you didn't want me to. It was beautiful out there."

"Even with the spider?"

She laughed and punched him in the arm. "Even then. Besides, I know you'll save me. After you look your fill."

"I'll never look my fill, but I will take any opportunity I can get to stare at your body."

He crossed the room to pick his cell up. His limp, while almost non-existent, still remained. He'd done well with it, not that a limp would bother her but she knew it did him.

"When do you want to leave?" he asked.

The joy on his face was what had been missing. She knew he needed to go back and see those he considered family. He'd gone to Ireland for a two week trip and that had vastly improved his attitude. Still it wasn't those who surrounded him at the cabin.

"We can go tonight if you want. I have two weeks off work so it's up to you. My parents are celebrating their anniversary over in Paris so no conflicts there."

"After the fireworks then."

"Make the arrangements and I'll go tell Terri we're leaving. She'll keep an eye on the place."

"I'll get our flights and let Martin know we're coming in. He'll stock the cabin."

She kissed him then walked over to Terri's.

"Hey, girl. Weren't you down at the lake?"

She shrugged as Terri hooted. "Hush. Listen, we're going to head to his cabin. Can you get my mail for me and keep an eye on the place?"

"Ohh, some of that cabin loving. Sounds good. Of course I can. How long are you going for?"

"I have only two weeks off so I'll be back before the end of that. I'm not sure when he's coming back."

Terri paused before jerking her inside and slamming the door behind her. "What's going on with you?"

"Nothing. I'm fine."

Terri crossed her arms and lifted an eyebrow. Caro told her about Jasmine and she grunted but didn't say anything until she had finished.

"And?"

"And what, Terri? That's it."

She leaned close and sniffed. "I smell a liar. I've known you since we were both freshmen on this campus. We roomed together and have become inseparable. Do you think I don't know when you're lying to me?"

"You're reaching. I'm fine."

Terri made a face. "Right. Of course you are." She reached around her and opened the door. "Have a great trip and let me know when you're back."

"Will do. Thanks, Terri."

"Anytime, hon. Will we see you tonight at the fireworks?"

"Oh sure. We're on our way back down there. We'll save you a seat."

"Great. We'll be by closer to the start. He doesn't get off work until later."

"Not a problem. See you then." She walked back to her place and paused with her hand on the doorknob. Peering over her shoulder she found Terri watching her with a knowing expression on her face. Caro stuck her tongue out and vanished inside her place.

"All set?"

"We're on the Red Eye." Declan went to her side and held her. "Are you sure you want to do this?"

"Yes. Why is everyone asking me if I'm sure and if nothing is wrong?"

He backed off. "Okay. Just wanted to make sure."

"I'll be packing my bag." She walked by him to the bedroom. He joined her about five minutes later and got his own luggage ready. Then together they made their way down and back out into the summer afternoon. Hand in hand they strolled along State Street, not rushing, just ambling as they took in all the stores.

They claimed their spot on the grass at dusk and he held her close during the fireworks display. Next to them were Terri and her boyfriend. The four of them went out for a late drink after, then went their separate ways, Terri back to the apartment with her boyfriend and Caro to the airport with Declan.

* * * *

Declan stood over Caro in nothing but his jeans as the woman he loved slumbered. They'd been here for three days now and he was more than happy to be back. Martin had set them up perfectly, even putting the phone back in. They'd not gone to see anyone yet, opting instead to stay there, be just the two of them.

Knowing that wouldn't last and people would be coming to see them, he let her sleep as long as she needed. Or wished. Scratching his chest, he turned and walked from the room. In the kitchen he began making pancakes. She still hadn't woken by the time they were finished so he ate alone. He left her a note and put the other pancakes in the oven to say warm.

He was out in the shed when her shadow fell over him. Rolling the creeper out from below the Jeep he stared up at her.

"Hey," she said.

"Hey, yourself. Get enough sleep?"

"Must be the mountain air." She tucked a curl behind one ear. "Sorry for sleeping so long."

"No need to apologize, Caro. This is a vacation. You want to sleep. You get to sleep. No rules."

"I think there should be one or two."

"Like?"

"Like I don't wake up with a vibrator by me but no man."

"It was in the bed with both of us last night. I don't know what happened for it to be by you specifically."

She rolled her eyes and pulled her hair up into a ponytail. "Whatever. Next time, wake me up."

"Will do. And I'll be sure to enlist its help again." He watched her pupils dilate. She loved him and vibrator together and to be truthful, so did he.

"Now, what can I do to help?"

"Just changing oil. I'll be done in five minutes if you'd like to go into town after that. I know Tasha would like to see you."

Indecision was blatant on her face and he sat up then beckoned to her. She crouched by him and he ran the back of his hand along her face. "They aren't going to hold anything against you, Caro. It wasn't your doing."

"My twin fucked her husband. How will she look at me in any way but as a home wrecker."

"She will, trust me."

A light shrug. "Okay."

* * * *

Declan stared at the woman sleeping on his shoulder as they flew back across the country. They'd been at his cabin for ten days. The time had flown by and while he regretted leaving, part of him was looking forward to getting back to Madison.

By all appearances, it seemed Caro had had a great time out there as well. She and Tasha had been nearly inseparable. Her day hours had been taken up by Tasha but the nights... The nights had belonged to him.

He wouldn't have had it any other way. Caro was a giving and passionate lover. Departing the plane didn't take too long and they sat together while waiting for their luggage. They stopped at an all-night diner on their way back to the apartment. His phone rang as they entered her place, and he shut the door behind them.

"Hello?" he said, carrying their bags to the bedroom.

"McBride."

"LT, what's up?"

"I didn't wake you, did I?"

"No, we just got in. Something I can do for you?"

"Yeah. Have time to come down here for a couple days? We'll pay for your ticket."

He narrowed his gaze. "What's this about?"

Declan felt Caro behind him and turned to give her a smile, shaking his head no when she asked if he needed privacy.

"I'd feel better talking to you about this in person as opposed to over the phone."

"Okay. When's the flight?"

"How soon can you get to the airport?"

* * * *

"I'll have to check with Caro on this, LT." Declan reclined back in the chair he occupied.

"You? Checking with a woman about your career?"

"That woman is my future. I don't want to be here if she's in Madison. Nope, I'm going to have to talk to her about it." He tapped his fingers on the file. "I appreciate the thought, however."

"It's a chance to put the uniform on again."

"It's a glorified desk job, LT. Let's not kid ourselves. I left because I didn't want to ride a desk."

"It's good money, McBride, and you'd be helping out the department. The officers. The brotherhood."

"I read it, LT. Like I said, I have to talk to Caro about it."

The man stood up. "So call her." He walked out.

He pulled out his phone and pressed the button to call her.

"Hello?"

"Hey, baby."

"Declan, how's Atlanta?"

He tipped his head from side to side. "It's interesting. LT offered me a job."

She squealed, excitement pouring from her. "How wonderful, Declan. I know you've missed wearing a uniform. What's the job?"

"I'm basically at a desk but they'd call me a liaison. I guess some of the rookies and lower members of the brotherhood have been feeling undervalued and don't know who to talk to about problems without going to IA."

"So you'd be the one they went to first and if you suggest they head to someone further up the chain they would do so?"

"Pretty much." He scratched his chin. "I have the years to get respect even if I'm not a detective."

"When do you start?"

He blinked and sat forward. "You don't have a problem with me taking this?"

Silence met him and he was about to ask again when she spoke. "Why would I have a problem with you doing what you loved to do?"

"What about us?"

"What about us?"

"Isn't that going to make things difficult?"

"People do have long-distance relationships, Declan. Unless you think being that close to Jac—"

"Don't," he growled. "Don't even go there."

"Then I don't see what the problem is."

"You, my love, are very pragmatic."

"Some would say that."

"I just did."

"Listen to me, Declan. Whether you are here with me in person or we are communicating by phone, that's not going to change my love for you. I want, no, *need* you to be happy as well. Think about it. If this is what you want to do then you have not only my support but my blessing if that makes you feel better. I have to go back into the lab now. Love you." She hung up.

"Love you too," he told the air as he placed the phone back on the table.

LT must have been watching him from outside for he came back in and sat across from him. "So, what'd she say?"

"To do what makes me happy."

Bushy eyebrows rose. "And that would be?"

"Let's give it a trial run."

Epilogue

She missed him. There was no denying that. Caro sipped her drink as she walked through the students who raced from class to class. She was done for the day. Three broken beakers was her clue to take some time off.

She made her way down to Memorial Union and found a seat on the Terrace at one of the brightly colored starburst chairs. She rested her chin on her hand and stared out over Lake Mendota. Water skiers went by, there were swimmers, and even some practicing for rowing.

"I need to call him," she said as she debated getting up and going for some Babcock ice cream.

"Someone important?"

She turned in time to see Declan lowering himself into one of the chairs beside hers, two ice creams in his hand.

"Declan."

"Give us a kiss, woman, I haven't seen you in weeks."

She did as he'd ordered, closing her eyes at the wealth of emotions that coursed through her. Tears pricked her eyes and she willed them away. "What are you doing here?"

"You told me to do what I thought was best. I tried the job there and it wasn't bad, not like being on the street but not horrible. Didn't matter, though. You weren't there when I went home. Or when I got up in the mornings. What's best for me, Caro, is you. I want to be with you. Be that here or wherever."

Damn traitorous tears leaked free. He shoved a cone — hers, she knew by the chocolate ice cream — into her hand and wiped her tears away with his thumb.

"Baby, what's wrong? Why are you crying?"

"No reason."

"Caro." He wiped more tears.

"I'm pregnant."

His face blanked before he swallowed a few times. "Pregnant?"

"Yes. I got the news this morning. Dropped stuff all day at the lab so came down here to try and figure out how I was going to break the news to you. Then you showed up here, with ice cream and those damn words which made me cry. This is your fault."

His grin wasn't what she had been expecting, that was for sure. "Anyone want two ice cream cones?" he hollered. Two students took them and he gathered her tight in his arms. "You're damn right this is my fault, Caro. I got you pregnant and I plan on marrying you."

"But you want to be a cop and be in Atlanta. If I'm pregnant you'll feel obligat—"

His lips cut off her protest. He didn't let up on the pressure until she sagged against him.

"Don't go there, woman. I love you. I came back because I missed you. You're carrying our baby, we will be married and this child will be born a McBride. When that happens, we'll celebrate and give him lots of siblings to play with."

He smoothed his thumb along her cheek. "I am not letting you go, Caro. It may have been because of an assumed identity that brought us together but we're together and dammit, woman, I'm keeping you. You're good for me. I'll work here. I don't care doing what, so long as we're together. What do you say? Will you marry me?"

The Terrace had long since fallen silent as everyone gathered there stared at her. Waiting for an answer.

A chant of "Say yes" began and rose as more and more people picked it up.

She bit the inside of her lower lip and nodded her head. "Yes."

Declan held up his hand looking for silence. He got it. "What was that?" he asked again.

"Yes," she cried out. "Yes I'll marry you, Declan McBride."

The crowd around them gave a resounding cheer. Declan clasped his hands on her face and, with his tender grip, leaned in close and whispered, "I love you, Carolyn. From now until beyond forever."

When his lips met hers, Caro knew she'd found that which had been missing from her life. Full acceptance of the man's love beside her. They would have a family. They would be a family and nothing would ever change that. Her best day, in the city she loved more than anything, with the man who meant the world to her. How could anything get better than this?

Declan placed one hand over her belly as if protecting the life she carried within her. And she knew when this perfection would get better. The day their child arrived in the world. She didn't need anything more. She had it all.

About the Author

USA TODAY BESTSELLING AUTHOR

Aliyah Burke is an avid reader and is never far from pen and paper (or the computer). She is married to a career military man, and they have a German Shepherd, two Borzois, and a DSH cat. Her days are spent sharing her time between work, writing, and dog training.

Aliyah Burke loves to hear from readers. You can find her contact information, website details and author profile page at http://www.totallybound.com.

Totally Bound Publishing

Home of Erotic Romance